KNIGHT OF HAVOC

THE KNIGHTS OF THE ANARCHY
(BOOK 3)

SHERRY EWING

ARE YOU SIGNED UP FOR DRAGONBLADE'S BLOG?

You'll get the latest news and information on exclusive giveaways, exclusive excerpts, coming releases, sales, free books, cover reveals and more.

Check out our complete list of authors, too!

No spam, no junk. That's a promise!

Sign Up Here

www.dragonbladepublishing.com

Dearest Reader;

Thank you for your support of a small press. At Dragonblade Publishing, we strive to bring you the highest quality Historical Romance from some of the best authors in the business. Without your support, there is no 'us', so we sincerely hope you adore these stories and find some new favorite authors along the way.

Happy Reading!

CEO, Dragonblade Publishing

ADDITIONAL DRAGONBLADE BOOKS BY AUTHOR SHERRY EWING

The Knights of the Anarchy Series
Knight of Darkness (Book 1)
Knight of Chaos (Book 2)
Knight of Havoc (Book 3)

The Lyon's Den Series
To Claim a Lyon's Heart
The Lyon and His Promise

Knight of Havoc:
The Knights of the Anarchy (Book Three)
By Sherry Ewing

One lone knight. One strongminded maiden. When duty wars with love at first sight, which will win?

Long ago, Reynard Norwood loved deeply, but the lady died, and he vowed never to love again. On a mission for the Empress Matilda, he finds a lady worthy of love. She is barely surviving. How can he leave her? But how can he break his vow to the dead? Torn between loyalty to a ghost and following his heart, he must still make certain that the living lady is safe and secure.

The life of Lady Elysande Thorburn of Blackmore has been in turmoil since King Stephen and his men laid siege to her home. With few resources, she must care for an ailing grandfather and meet her responsibilities to those loyal to the household. Her options for survival are running out. One of Empress Matilda's knights arrives at her weakest moment. He's determined she must leave with him, but she's just as determined to stay.

Nothing about their relationship is simple, least of all the attraction each has for the other. As havoc and conflicting demands surround them, is love even possible?

DEDICATION

For my cousin Kerry…

The miles may keep us apart, but I'm so happy we found each
other again.
I love you very much. This one is for you.

PROLOGUE

IN A TIME known today as The Anarchy, England was torn between two enemies, each claiming a right to the throne. Some of England's nobles pledged their allegiance to Stephen and declared him king whilst others cast their fate with Empress Matilda, the daughter of Henry I. Such unrest placed most of the country into a state of civil war lasting for almost a score of years. Many knights bore the burden of fighting for either side, each determined to win the land for whomever they served.

Amongst such knights were three brothers and another knight who was the brother of their heart. These four swore their loyalty to fight for the Empress Matilda and her rightful claim to England's crown. The Norwood brothers were close in age. Wymar was the eldest and jumped at the chance to swear his oath of fealty to the Empress, especially after their parents were killed when Stephen laid siege to their home, Brockenhurst Castle. Ousted from the only home they had known six years ago, Wymar plunged his brothers into the middle of war all in the hopes of having the Empress crowned queen. He prayed, in return for his service, she would bestow upon him the return of his lands and his title, and that she would name him her champion knight.

Theobald was next and the peacekeeper amongst them. He was used to following his eldest brother no matter that he would prefer to sit in front of a fire to rest his weary feet with a mug of ale in his hand. Reynard, the youngest, was always attempting to prove his worth even when the odds were stacked against him. He was more like his eldest brother than he would ever admit, even to himself. He had no desire to wed after losing the woman he loved in his youth. And Richard, the brother of their heart, fought beside them all in support of the empress's cause.

The four of them swore to remain together as a family as they had no one else besides each other. But things changed as the war progressed. The first change was when Brockenhurst and Wymar's titles were restored. Wymar had wed, and then Theobald had, as well. Both were now settling into wedded bliss and holding estates in the empress's name. This left Reynard and Richard to continue to follow the empress until they, too, were released from their service.

Every tale has a beginning, a middle and an end for the knights of the Anarchy. This is Reynard's story…

CHAPTER ONE

Gloucester, England
October, 1141

S IR REYNARD NORWOOD stood along the wall of the solar with several other knights waiting to be noticed. He was not used to being idle and doing nothing but feasting and paying attention to the women at court. *Court life!* Bah! He fumed. He was not cut out for the flirtatious advances of the women who did everything in their power to persuade him to bed them. 'Twas not that he was not tempted a time or two... He was, after all, only human, but they wanted more from him than just a one-night tumble in their bed.

He had some monies stored away from the time he had been in service to the Empress. Yet 'twas not enough to see him live a comfortable life or ensure an estate of his own. As a younger son, he was not set to inherit. For Reynard to earn land, he had surmised long ago that such an outcome could only be accomplished by the graciousness of the Empress granting him something in his own name. The other alternative was to marry someone landed. He grimaced, thinking again of the grasping women of court. Now that the Norwood good name had been restored, 'twas as though every woman in all of England wished to wed him. As for himself, he had no wish to wed. Not anymore.

A brief vision of a beautiful young girl flitted across his mind. *Lady Johanna...* Her hair had been as black at the midnight sky and she'd had eyes so green they rivaled a forest after a rainfall.

She had been everything to him and he would have pledged her his troth if he had been given the opportunity. Aye… he had been so in love with her despite their age. Had he really been but ten and seven? Six years seemed like a lifetime ago and he heaved a heavy sigh as the memories once more plagued him.

Johanna lived on the borders of their land. Their union would have made both their parents happy and would have ensured the couple would take over Johanna's castle once her parents were one day gone from this world. Reynard remembered when he received word that she had taken ill. He barely had time to saddle his horse and arrive at their gates. But he had been too late. She had perished from an illness, and he had been lucky that he, too, had not taken ill. He had vowed that day he would guard his heart against another woman attempting to take Johanna's place.

Reynard had barely been given any time to mourn her loss before Brockenhurst was put under siege by King Stephen's men. Their father—the parent who had raised them alone after the death of their mother bringing Reynard into the world—had told them to gather what they could and escape through the secret tunnel whilst he held off the men to give Reynard and his brothers time to reach safety. 'Twas the last time they had seen him alive. The Norwood brothers lost more than their home that day. They had lost their beloved father who had been beheaded after he refused to renounce his allegiance to Empress Matilda.

His brief return to Brockenhurst to witness his older brother Wymar's wedding to the Lady of Norwich proved his brother had his work cut out ahead of him to restore the estate to its former glory. The keep, thank the heavens, had remained intact but many of the outer buildings, along with the stone wall surrounding the estate, were in need of heavy repairs. 'Twould be years before all would be returned to what it once was.

His other brother, Theobald, was also now wed to a woman who turned out to be of noble birth—something that had been a surprise even to the lady in question. Who would have known when his brother found a woman in the forest that she would turn out to be the missing heiress to Calbridge Castle? His brothers were lucky men, having fallen in love with wives who were rich, beautiful, and skilled with swords, as well. Their happiness left Reynard wondering if love would ever find him again.

He scowled, thinking of being bound to one woman for the rest of his life. He was still young and up to now, he had thought of little other than the pleasures life could bring him and the monies that would line his coffers with the empress's support. But one day the war would end, and what then? Would he not be required to wed as well? The empress appeared to have a plan for all the Norwood brothers, including Lord Richard Grancourt who was a much a part of his family as any other.

When had their plan to stay together as a family fallen apart? Mayhap 'twas the moment Wymar was restored his title and Brockenhurst returned to its rightful owner. Once that had happened, their lives had not been the same. Battling for the empress to be the rightful queen of England had been ingrained in their souls and Reynard had willingly followed his brothers' lead at the Battles of Lincoln and Winchester. But now… he gave a heavy sigh. He was tired of doing nothing but waiting.

"Stop fidgeting, Reynard," Richard hissed as he stood next to him.

"I am anxious," Reynard replied. "I hate doing nothing but listening to whatever may happen next to affect my life."

"She does nothing but what is best for her cause. You know that," Richard replied whilst he continued to stand there as though he was a marble statue.

"I just want some kind of action to relieve this infernal boredom," Reynard said, swiping his hand through his dark brown hair.

An amused chuckle left Richard. "Be careful what you ask for."

Reynard's gaze went across the room to the empress, who was visibly agitated. She argued with the men who offered their opinions on the next course of action, laying out their options. There were not many. Winchester had been her attempt to atone for her loss of London. She had barely made it to her half-brother's estate in Gloucester. Her army was defeated and had become scattered. Her coffers were near empty, making Reynard wonder if perchance he may not be rewarded someday as handsomely as he had hoped.

"There must be another way! I cannot believe they are holding Earl Robert as a prisoner. How the devil was he even caught?" Empress Matilda bellowed, banging her fists upon the table.

"I do not see what else can be done, my Empress," Reginald de Dunstanville said with a slight bow.

"I cannot give up Stephen as my hostage. If I were to do so, I would give up any bargaining power that I still hold," she replied angrily as she began to pace again.

"If you wish to see your half-brother released from his own captivity, then you will have to yield to their demands."

"I must have Robert returned," she growled in frustration, "else any further campaigns will be for naught. I will never be able to take the throne without Robert's assistance."

One of the empress's barons chimed in. "'Twill be the best solution," Brian fitz Count answered.

"Very well. We shall see that Stephen is released from Bristol and send word to Queen Matilda that in return, I demand Robert's release. To expedite the matter, we can make the exchange in Winchester."

"Who will you send for such an important mission? Not only must you send someone who can see that the usurper does not escape but you must needs find someone trustworthy to see to the earl's well-being."

Reynard's attention went to the empress and their eyes met across the room.

"Norwood," she called out.

"Aye, my Empress," Reynard answered, stepping forward.

"I shall task you with the honor of exchanging my brother the

Earl of Gloucester for the usurper Stephen. Make your way to Winchester with a contingent of men after securing the false king from Bristol. In the meantime, we will make our way to Oxford, and you can meet up with us there after the prisoners are exchanged."

Reynard bowed. "As you wish, Empress Matilda." Reynard turned and went to stand before Richard. "Care for a little adventure?"

A smirk lit Richard's face. "I thought you would never ask."

They two men softly chuckled and left the room to ready themselves for their travels. Reynard could only ponder what awaited them upon the open road.

CHAPTER TWO

Blackmore Castle
Outside of Bristol, England

L ADY ELYSANDE THORBURN of Blackmore took hold of the rope in a firm grip and pulled. The cow bellowed in protest, and she yanked harder trying to get the animal to move. With her livestock scattered, she had been only too happy when she had come across this animal chewing its cud in a field. If she could only get the stubborn beast back to what was left of her stables, she would at least have fresh milk. There was not much else left.

She let the rope go slack. Any effort on her part to have this animal agree to being led had gotten her nowhere. She crossed the distance and ran her gloved fingers over the animal whilst staring into its soft brown eyes. She laid her forehead on its neck in defeat.

"Please, God, help me," she whispered softly hoping that her plea to a higher being might be heard.

As if in answer to her prayer, the cow finally stepped forward. Elysande raised her eyes heavenward and gave a silent word of thanks. With the slightest of tugs, she and the animal began walking back toward the castle. The beast would at least be fed once inside the barn. Aye... she still had enough hay for the cow and grain for the few chickens she had managed to return to the coop. Any other livestock had been slaughtered by Stephen's army when they came through the area, rampaging in protest that their king had been taken and held in Bristol.

She scowled at the memory but was thankful she had hidden herself away and had not been a part of the destruction they had left in their aftermath. They had ransacked whatever had remained of the village. What had been left of her fields after the harvest had been burned as had her outbuildings. Her serfs had either been captured or killed and she had been left to bury the bodies. She had herself, a handful of servants, and her elderly grandfather to take care of since her parents had been staying at one of their estates in Normandy. She had sent word months ago of her plight, but the message may have been delayed or lost since she had had no word of their return. Not that they would be of much help rather than burdening her further. Nay... Blackmore was hers and her parents had been mostly absent from her life.

Her situation was grim, and she had no idea how she would continue to feed not only herself but those who had remained loyal to her household. And her ailing grandfather... no one should live out their last days starving. She was already aware that he was not long for this world.

She reached the outskirts of Blackmore wishing with all her might that she would open her eyes to find that this had all been but a horrible nightmare. But the view before her did not miraculously change from the one she now gazed upon. The barbican gate with its portcullis was a shambles. The stone walls were now in need of repair, but both were far beyond her capabilities and those of her household servants. She would need a mason along with the manpower to work the heavy stones back into place. The knights who had guarded the keep had done their best, but they had been no match for an army bent on destroying all in their path. Their heavy machinery of war had seen to what little there was to the perimeter of her home. She should be thankful the keep was still in one piece.

Leading the cow into the stable and then a stall, she left the animal after ensuring she was fed. She had barely made her way through the inner bailey before her maid, Olive, ran down from the steps of the keep. Her worried frown made Elysande run the remaining distance to reach her. She grasped the maid's hands.

"What has happened?" Elysande urged whilst fearing the worse.

"'Tis your grandfather. You must come quickly, milady," Olive replied.

Hearing her grandfather needed her, she left her maid behind whilst racing into the keep and making her way up through the turret. The circular stairs slowed down her pace but once she reached the second floor where her grandsire's bedchamber was located, she once more ran down the passageway. His door was ajar, and she pushed the portal open. That the castle priest was inside caused Elysande to choke back her tears.

"Grandfather," she called whilst rushing to his side. She took his cool frail hand and brought it up to her cheek. One boney finger traced the tear that slid unbidden down her face.

"Ah, my sweet granddaughter. How I wish I could keep death from my door. But he has come for me and will wait no longer," Barnabus wheezed out before a coughing fit made Elysande reach for a cup on the table next to his bed. She made an attempt to get him to drink once he caught his breath again, but he waved the chalice away.

"Death cannot take you from me, Grandfather. He will have to wait," she insisted. Olive had arrived and she went to grab a wooden stool and brought it to the side of the bed. Elysande took a seat.

"He has waited long enough, child. If only your parents had returned from Normandy so I would know I was leaving you in their care. Now you will be alone," he whispered looking about the room as if her parents would miraculously appear.

"She will not be left alone, Sir Barnabus." A deep baritone voice with a French accent called out from the doorway. A small smile lit Elysande's lips.

"You see, Grandfather? Sir Hawke de Challon is still here watching over me," she answered whilst the priest continued to lift up prayers on her grandfather's behalf.

"He is not the same as your parents or a husband, Elysande, but I suppose he will have to do," he murmured whilst keeping his gaze upon her.

Hawke stepped forward and gave a slight bow. "I have promised to protect this lady from the day of my first service in this household. Nothing will change that, Sir Barnabus."

A heavy sigh left the man lying in the bed and he closed his eyes at Hawke's words. 'Twas as though any energy he still had left him knowing she would be taken care of. "Good. Good," he answered before he turned pale blue eyes in her direction. "You have been a blessing in my life, child. Never forget that you are loved." He gave her a weak smile before heaving one last sigh as his final breath left him.

"Grandfather!" she sobbed but 'twas of no use. He was now gone, and she had no idea how she was to go on in this world without his guidance.

A strong arm came around her shoulders and pulled her from the stool. "Come, Elysande. You have done enough for one day. Let the priest give your grandfather his final prayers. You must needs rest. Olive, come see to your lady's comfort in her chambers," Hawke said ushering her toward the door. Olive went around them and disappeared down the corridor.

Elysande looked over her shoulder for one last look at her grandfather whilst there was still the slight bit of color to his skin. "I will need to see to his grave."

"Nay," Hawke replied. "I will see to it myself along with sending a servant downstairs to the kitchen to ensure there is an evening meal for you to fill your belly. When was the last time you ate?"

She shrugged. "Does it matter?"

"Aye, *ma petite*, it does. I will not have you wasting away whilst you give your meager portions of food to others. You will do yourself no good if you do not retain your strength."

They left the bedchamber and made their way to the turret,

climbing the stairs to the fourth floor where her own room was located. "There is too much work for me to do still, Hawke. There is no time to rest."

"For today, you are finished, my lady," Hawke insisted.

"Ordering me about, are you, Hawke?" she managed to tease. She peered up into his green eyes. His blond-brown hair hung in soft waves to his shoulders. There was a time in her youth where she thought she had been in love with this handsome Frenchman, not that she was old at only a score of years. But five years was a long time to hold an affection for someone when she knew her parents would never approve and she had finally given up on any notion of finding love with the captain of her guard.

A slight chuckle left him, not that there was anything to be merry about. "At least for the remainder of the day, my lady," he murmured whilst opening the portal to her bedchamber. Olive had already turned down the coverlets and waited for Hawke to depart.

"You will personally see to his grave?" she asked stepping farther into the room before turning around to face him.

"Aye, Elysande, I will see to it personally," he assured her before giving her a bow and taking his leave, shutting the door behind him.

Elysande went to the bed to pull the covers back up. "'Tis too early in the afternoon to climb into bed, Olive. I will just take my ease with a short rest. You can return when 'tis time for the evening meal unless I am already downstairs in the hall," she said as the weight of what she had lost this day fell upon her.

She waved her maid away and once she was left in the privacy of her bedchamber, she climbed on top of the coverlets and the softness of her bed. For once, she would not think of the responsibilities that awaited her outside of this door. Instead, she dreamed of a carefree life where her parents doted upon her, and suitors came to call who would take her breath away. If only life were that simple.

❖

CHAPTER THREE

REYNARD CHECKED THE saddle straps of his horse one last time. All was in order. He only awaited on Richard who had his hands full with his sister, Beatrix.

She stomped her foot. "You cannot leave me here, Richard. Why, what if some man attempts to take advantage of me? Who will defend my honor if you are not here?" she complained bitterly.

Richard continued to see to his horse before he finally turned his attention to his sister. "I doubt any man could withstand your sharp tongue. You will behave yourself and attend the empress as is required of you. That is your duty. Besides, you will soon be on your way to Oxford. I expect you to stay out of trouble," he answered before placing a kiss upon her cheek. He then put his foot into the stirrup and settled into the saddle. "Do not make me regret leaving you alone."

"You shall be sorry the moment you leave Gloucester's gates," she fumed, crossing her arms over her chest.

"Heaven help me! How I wish our parents were here at court instead of back home at Lyndhurst," Richard uttered, turning his attention to Reynard. "Can you say something to her to make her behave?"

A burst of laughter left Reynard. "You think I have some kind of control over her?"

"One can only hope," Richard said with a sigh. "Do something about her, Reynard."

"She is *your* sister," he chuckled.

"But you are like her brother as well. Mayhap you will have some kind of an influence over her since you are of the same age." Richard pulled on the reins turning his horse around. "Behave yourself, sister, and I will see you soon in Oxford."

Beatrix stuck out her tongue before composing her features to face Reynard. "I suppose you think to control me, too, before you leave for Bristol," she said with a frown, "as if you ever could."

"I would not dare," Reynard replied with a slight smile. She appeared so forlorn he felt a moment of pity toward the younger woman who, as Richard had just said, was like the sister he never had. "I know how you enjoy being the center of attention and I would think that you would have more freedom without your brother watching your every move. What has you so upset, Beatrix?"

She widened her eyes as though she were surprised that he could read her so easily. She shrugged and gave a sigh. "I have no friends here, Reynard. No one to confide in or have a friendly conversation. The other women of court only think of me as a lady in waiting to the empress with special privileges. They do not see me for who I am."

He gave her a small grin of understanding. "The cattiness of other women never bothered you before."

"Mayhap not, but their snobbish ways bother me now," she fumed with a stamp of her foot.

"I am certain you will put them in their place by the time we see you again," Reynard teased her, noticing the determined look that filled her eyes.

"You, too, will regret leaving me to my own devices. Why, I shall flirt my way through all the men left here at court. 'Twill teach both you and Richard a lesson for leaving me behind," she said batting her eyes at him and ruining the brief bit of pity he had for her.

Reynard went to her and kissed both of her cheeks. Returning to his horse, he settled into the saddle before reaching for his leather gloves and donning them. He took up the reins. "Do as you must, Beatrix, but in the end, you are the one who will pay the price for your ruination."

"Who said I will be ruined? I am looking for a husband," she fumed, her tone sounding on the brink of hysterics. "I do not know why I am having to explain myself to you anyway. We are of the same age, and I hardly answer to you anymore than I answer to your brothers."

"We have always kept your best interest in our hearts, and you know it, Beatrix. Continue on as you have claimed, and you will find yourself with a babe in your belly if your plan is to flirt your way through court. In the end, you will not have a husband to claim but a bastard child," he replied whilst giving her a look of the importance of his words.

"Then do not leave me here!" She stomped her foot once again.

"Your attempt to threaten us to keep us from leaving you here is useless. The empress herself has asked you to attend her but there are plenty of reasons like your safety to not travel with us into the unknown. We have no idea what may lie ahead for us in Bristol and Winchester."

"Bah!" she said with a wave of her hand. "I would be far better off traveling with you and my brother, and you know it, Reynard," she said. She placed her hands on her hips. "Say the word and I will have my horse saddled to ride with you."

"I will not gainsay your brother or our empress, whom you must answer to, Beatrix. As Richard told you, behave yourself until we see you again at Oxford. Surely you can keep yourself respectfully amused until then. I am certain you will be complaining about us keeping a watchful eye over you in no time."

"You are just as mean as my brother. I hate you both. Begone with you then," she scolded before turning her back on him and walking away.

Reynard sighed before pulling on the reins of his horse and

setting the beast into motion. The other knights who were to travel with him were already making their way through the barbican gate.

He kicked his steed into a trot to catch up to where Richard rode in the procession of knights. There were three others whom he had fought besides during the rout of Winchester: Blake Kennarde, Oswin Woodwarde, and Kingsley Goodee had also sworn their allegiance to the empress and Reynard was happy to have them as additional company on their travels.

The morning gave way to early afternoon as the party continued to make their way toward Bristol. As soon as they had the false king in hand, they would continue on to make the prisoner exchange in Winchester. Reynard continued to keep his eyes upon the road and watch the trees for a possible ambush, but all was far too quiet.

Oswin finally inched his steed closer to Reynard. "Did you survive her sharp tongue?" he teased as though they had only just left Beatrix behind.

Reynard smirked. "That girl will need someone with a fair amount of patience to deal with everything that is... well... Beatrix."

Blake's horse trotted forward, and he looked over his shoulder to stare upon the men with a wicked smile. "I would be happy to take up the challenge."

"Aye! Richard's sister is a beauty," Kingsley chimed in.

A low growl-like sound left Richard. "You shall all stay away from my sister," he warned, causing the men to laugh.

Reynard looked ahead, trying to keep a straight face but failed. "They are all worthy of her. Titled with lands to call their own. What more could you want for Beatrix?" he asked, curious as to Richard's answer.

"A stable life with someone who is not following an army might be a start," Richard said, casting a warning glance toward those who rode nearby.

"And what about love? Do you not wish her to find love,

Richard?" Oswin inquired with a knowing smile.

Richard nodded. "That would be ideal but knowing my sister I would be happy if she could find a common accord with this unknown man and not want to scratch his eyes out. She has quite the temper when provoked."

Blake laughed. "Again… sounds like a challenge," he taunted which earned him a warning glare from Oswin. "What? Do you fancy her?"

Oswin became quiet whilst the friends all stared upon him.

"*God's Blood*! He does care for the fair Lady Beatrix," Kingsley called, causing his voice to echo into the distance.

"*Sod off*, Goodee," Oswin huffed before kicking his heels into the side of his horse and trotting ahead.

"I guess I must beg off in pursing her, then. I certainly do not wish to get in the way of Oswin's claim," Blake replied in a tart retort.

Richard scowled. "No one is pursing anything where my sister is concerned."

"Best let the matter rest, men," Reynard finally chimed in knowing Richard was barely holding onto his temper. "I shall go scout ahead."

Richard nodded and sent Reynard off with a wave of his hand. Reynard left the men behind as he galloped ahead of their party. He slowed his mount when he smelled smoke somewhere off in the distance. 'Twas still several miles more until they reached their destination, causing Reynard to wonder what was close by.

Shielding his eyes from the sun, he briefly caught sight of a plume of dark grey smoke above the tree line. With a cluck of his tongue, he sent his horse forward again in the general direction. The usurper's men had been ransacking all in its path and Reynard could only assume some village was in need of aid.

But when he came upon what was left, he was well aware that the only aid he might be giving would be to bury their dead. 'Twould be years before the land recovered. His horse picked its way carefully over the debris whilst Reynard gazed ahead to see the keep rising above what was left of the curtain wall. A sound of weeping caused him to stop once more to gain his bearings and to determine where the cry of anguish originated from. A small fence showed the outline of a cemetery and Reynard pulled on the reins to have the horse head in that direction.

The sound of weeping grew louder as he drew near, and Reynard dropped down to the ground. He looped the reins over his horse's head and tied the steed to the fence. With a pat on its neck, he entered the small cemetery, wondering how the fence had remained intact. But he was more concerned with the woman who was so caught up in her grief that she did not hear him approach.

"May I offer you aid, my lady?" he asked gently, not wishing to scare her.

She jumped to her feet, swinging a small blade forward she had produced from her cloak. "Stay back!" she ordered looking past him to see if he was alone. She took several steps away from him.

Reynard held up his hands. "I mean you no harm."

"Ha! I have heard that before," she cried out wiping her eyes with the sleeve of her gown with her free hand. "Your kind have been here before and as you can see for yourself, there is not much left to pillage. Be gone with you!"

Reynard relaxed his stance. "As I just said, *mademoiselle*… I mean you no harm."

She eyed him, quizzically moving the dirk back and forth as though such a small blade could actually stop him if he wished to capture her. "To whom do you swear your allegiance?"

"The Empress Matilda," he stated as a matter of fact. "Did Stephen's men lay waste to your land?"

"Aye," she said still holding him at bay. "There may not be much left of Blackmore but 'tis still my home."

His gaze travelled to the keep rising in the distance. He frowned, wondering who this woman was. "You must know 'tis not safe to be left alone. These are trying times, my lady."

"Did I say I was alone?" she asked pointing the knife at him.

"I do not see anyone close by who is watching over you whilst you grieve. That alone tells me much." He took a hesitant step forward. "Mayhap we should introduce ourselves."

A sound escaped her… half laugh… half unladylike snort. "Introduce ourselves? Whatever for? I have no need for your name or anything else you might think to offer."

"I cannot in good conscience leave you alone to fend for yourself, my lady." He took another step forward whilst she backed away again.

"I am more than capable of taking care of myself," she fumed.

Reynard looked down upon the grave she had been weeping over and thought of another approach to gain her trust. "I am sorry for the loss of your loved one," he said. "I, too, have known much suffering at the loss of a parent."

Her eyes widened momentarily, and the blade lowered a fraction. "'Twas my grandfather. Who did you lose because of this blasted war for the throne?"

"My father… when my home Brockenhurst was overtaken by Stephen's men six years ago," he replied.

"I am sorry for your loss," she murmured quietly.

Reynard nodded his head. "No child should watch one of their parents die in such a ghastly manner. I pray your grandfather did not suffer."

"Nay… 'twas just his time so at least he did not die defending our home." She watched him with sorrowful blue eyes, and she seemed just as cautious as when he first came upon her.

He gave her a slight bow. "Sir Reynard Norwood of Brockenhurst. And you are?"

She took several breaths and finally lowered the blade. "Lady Elysande Thorburn of Blackmore."

"'Tis a pleasure to meet you, my lady, even though the circumstances are unusual," he said coming to stand next to her.

"Do you travel alone?" she asked whilst once more looking

past him.

"Nay. I but scouted ahead. The empress's men are currently headed to Bristol, and I am but a small part of that contingent. We are about her business," he said watching her carefully. He was unsure what to do with a lone woman. He felt honor-bound to offer her what aid he was capable of giving. 'Twas clear there was not much left to the land to sustain her for the coming winter. How was she to defend herself if she no longer had a garrison of knights? A need to see that she was safe filled him, though he was unsure why he was so concerned with a total stranger. Perchance the cause was because he knew of the suffering she was experiencing, given his own losses.

"I see…" Her words lingered in the air between them.

A gust of wind suddenly blew the hood of her cloak from her head and hair as black as the night swirled around her. The tresses took on a life of their own until she once again grabbed at the hood and pulled it over her head. Black hair… blue eyes… 'twas as though a vision of Lady Johanna came before him reminding him what he had lost and vowed never to find again.

'Twas, of course, a foolish promise to himself he had made in his youth, but he had remained guarded ever since. And yet, if the memories of Johanna's beauty could remain with his for this many years, 'twas nothing compared to the image of the woman who was standing before him. But now was not the time to dally with a woman, let alone one who was grieving the loss of her loved one.

He cleared his throat when the silence stretched between them. "What can I do to help you, Lady Elysande?" he asked, wondering what she truly had in the way of supplies to see to her immediate needs.

Her eyes widened before she shrugged. "There is not much for anyone to do, Sir Reynard," she replied apparently still wary of him. 'Twas hardly surprising, since he was nothing more than a stranger. "But I suppose you are hungry and, at the very least, I can feed you before you continue on your way." She began walking to the opening in the fence and Reynard followed her.

But as they made their way through the broken gate and Reynard viewed what remained of her interior buildings, he knew in his heart he could not leave a woman here to fend for herself with only meager supplies to sustain her. At least if she were to travel with the empress's men, they would see that she was fed until he could find better accommodations for her. Anything would be better than her current situation—which was beyond grim. The only question was now this… How would he convince the lady to travel with a complete stranger?

CHAPTER FOUR

ELYSANDE HELD THE platter of food as she made her way from
the kitchen and then through the great hall. The knight who
had found her grieving in Blackmore's cemetery came to a stand
and waited for her approach. She took a quick glance at the
meager offering on the tray she held. 'Twas not much in the way
of a meal but 'twas all she could offer the empress's knight. The
rabbit would not feed everyone who remained here anyway and
they would be stuck consuming porridge again for their evening
meal. Inwardly, she sighed. 'Twould not be the first night she
went to bed famished.

"Sit, Sir Reynard. There is no reason to stand on ceremony
here these days," she said, placing the platter before him. "I am
sorry I cannot offer you more but at least you will not leave here
hungry."

"You are too kind, my lady," Reynard replied as he waited for
her to take her place at the table. She sat on the bench across
from where he had been standing, keeping her distance since he
was a stranger. Thus far he had behaved as politely as any who
had come to her father's hall, but she did not know if this man
could be trusted.

A couple of servants stood near the kitchen entrance, ready to
be called if she needed aid, but she was unsure how much help
they would be. If there was ever a time that she wished she still
had even a handful of garrison knights, 'twas now. And where
was her captain? The one man she could always depend upon was

nowhere in sight. Elysande could only assume that some chore was keeping Hawke busy. 'Twas not like him to leave her unattended for long, and she would have thought he would have learned that a knight had arrived at Blackmore and come running to ensure her safety.

Sir Reynard finally took his seat and gazed upon the offering before him. "Will you not share this banquet with me?"

Banquet? A rabbit and a few root vegetables were hardly a banquet. She closed her eyes as memories flooded her mind of better times when the tables were laden with food of every kind, the hall filled with knights and their ladies merrily laughing whilst beautiful music played in the room from her mistrals.

"I am not hungry," she replied softly even though the smell of the meat made her head swim. 'Twas at that moment that her stomach made the unladylike rumble of protest.

Reynard quickly hid the slight smirk that lifted the corners of his lips. "I think you, too, are ravenous, my lady. I cannot, in good faith, eat this entire meal myself whilst a lady goes hungry." He stood and made his way around the table and sat next to her pushing the trencher between them.

Her eyes widened. "What are you doing?"

He pointed to the food between them. "Eat. 'Twill do you no good to starve yourself."

"I am not starving myself," she huffed.

"Mayhap not intentionally but by the sound your stomach just made, you have not supped in some time," he argued. He waited for her to make her choice of the food before them. "I will not start without you and the food grows cold the longer you wait."

"You are being awful bossy to someone who is only trying to feed one of the empress's men," she muttered even as the food began to make her mouth water.

A chuckle left him. "I have been told as much by many of my acquaintance," he declared before pointing to the trencher. "You first, my lady…"

His voice trailed away whilst he continued to wait for her decision. She threw him a glare since he forced her hand. "Very well," she uttered and took a small sample of the meat and began to chew.

The man next to her seemed satisfied since he, too, began to pick at the food they were clearly meant to share. The silence stretched between them since eating was far more important than witty conversation. This gave Elysande time to study the man seated beside her. Dark brown hair that could almost be deemed as black as her own fell in waves down to his shoulders. A chiseled nose similar to a Roman statue she once saw along with a firm square jaw. His eyes were the color of a stormy grey sky and there could be no doubt this man was a warrior knight for his body fit the image she had of a man defending the injustices of the world.

Heat rushed to her face and she bent her head forward so her hair would hide her embarrassment that she was thinking of this stranger's body. Of course, he had the body of a warrior. What a silly goose she was! He was as any other knight of her acquaintance, including those who once stood guard over this very castle. Hawke was just as fit, but the two men were as different as night was to day. One light and known to her and the other dark and possibly gloomy, although she could not say for certain what was currently causing the man next to her to frown when she stole a glimpse at him.

"You watch me most intently, my lady. Why?" he asked not looking away from the food before him. He reached for the chalice of wine she had earlier poured for him and he took a sip before he placed the goblet in front of her so they might share.

Her eyes widened for a second time. Had he knowingly settled the cup in such a way that if she were to lift it thusly, her lips would be where he had just taken a sip? Surely, 'twas a mistake and not meant as a lover's gesture. She cringed inside... a lover... he was far from that!

She reached for the goblet, turning it slightly, and took a sip.

If anything, it would wash down the food that seemed to stick in her throat. "You are displeased if the frown upon your brow says anything about you. Is the food not to your liking?" she finally asked. She tucked a lock of her hair behind her ear and turned on the bench to face him fully.

"The food is fine, although I feel as if I am taking this offering from those who need it more than I. Where are your attendants? Your guards?"

"Unfortunately, Stephen's army killed most of the men who used to guard Blackmore. Those who had still lived after the siege were taken as prisoners," she answered not revealing anything about Hawke.

"Surely your parents have not left you alone to your own devices now that your grandfather has passed on," he grumbled whilst those eyes the color of hard steel swept across her hall.

"Did I say I was alone?" she asked, worried now for her safety since she had not summoned Hawke or at least Olive to watch vigil over her and her guest. She'd had more than ample time whilst preparing his trencher to have one of the few remaining servants go and find her captain. Why had she not done so immediately? Her stupidity at such a move might be her downfall.

He reached over for the chalice, bringing him closer, and Elysande flinched, moving slightly away. She had been just short of being touched and for a moment their eyes met and held. She was not certain what she saw in those depths except perchance far too much concern as to her welfare and future. After he took a drink of his wine, his next words confirmed her worst fears.

"Nay. You did not say you were alone, but I fear you are more or less close to such an outcome. I do not see the normal number of servants rushing about a hall this size, no guards standing on what is left of your battlements as I approached. You, yourself, have said your parents are abroad which leaves me wondering what I am to do with you?" His gaze held hers and he tilted his head as if studying her further.

"Do with me?" she gasped. "There is nothing for you to do with or for me, sir. You shall finish your meal and be on your way."

"I can hardly leave a woman alone to fend for herself, my lady," he muttered whilst pushing the trencher in front of her.

She looked at the remainder of the food he had left her. She would not be able to get even a morsel past her lips in fear she might choke upon it. "There is no reason for you to be concerned for me. I assure you I am more than capable of seeing to my own needs."

He placed an elbow on the edge of the table. "And does that include what will happen to you the next time an army crosses your gates? Who will see to your safety then?"

"I do not need you or any other man to *see* to my safety. I can take care of myself!" she dared to repeat herself but clearly he was not impressed with her words.

His dark brow rose as if he was ready to challenge her words. "I admire your determination, my lady, honestly, I do. But as a knight of the empress, I am bound to offer my protection to any in need along my travels. Even now, those I travel with will arrive shortly since your castle is in the direct path on our way to Bristol."

"And should I fear those in her army as I did Stephen's?" she inquired tartly.

"I can vouch on the honor for several of the knights that are well known to me but who is to say some may not be as ethical," he declared frankly.

"Then if I have nothing to fear, there is no reason why I cannot stay here at my home," she murmured even as the dread of the unknown and how to survive the coming months consumed her.

"Let me be blunt, my lady, so you may come to the same conclusion as I have already done in the short time I have been here," he began before his hand ran over the back of his neck. "Your fields are gone, your outer walls destroyed. You are lucky the keep still stands but how will you feed yourself with the winter's approach? How many others are you responsible for? How will you feed any remaining servants if you stay here? Certainly, if they were not seeing to your welfare, they could return to the households of whatever family they might have close by. Or they could travel with us until we can find them a suitable place to live."

"I have been doing fine without you," she reiterated with a scowl.

"Starving yourself to feed others is to be commended but if you fall ill from fatigue, who, then, will take over their care?"

"Do you think I have not thought of this before? I assure you we were doing fine before your arrival. We shall be just as fine once you are gone." She stood as if this alone was a clue that he should take his leave of Blackmore. But his words did cause her to worry as to the welfare of her remaining people. She had no future plan that would keep them safe and fed. Sir Reynard was correct, as much as she hated to admit it, even to herself. She did not know how she would make it through the winter, but somehow she must try.

"You do not appear fine, Elysande," he said using her given name. "You should resign yourself to the fact you must leave here and ride with me and the empress's army. You will be safe in our company and she will find you a place in her court."

A distressed laugh escaped her. "Safe? You think I shall be safe with you? I do not even know you," she bellowed as the sound echoed in the empty hall.

"You do not have to *know* me, my lady, to know I shall keep my vow to see that you are well protected until you can one day return to your home." He stood. "I will give you time to think on the matter. In the meantime, I will see to my horse and sleep in the barn."

She stomped her foot. "You have eaten your fill. Now you can be on your way!"

He gave her a courtly bow that rivaled anything she had ever witnessed from those who tried to win her favor in her hall. "I shall leave as long as you plan to accompany me. I have given you a knight's vow that I will see you are protected. What kind of man would I be if I so readily dismissed it once given?"

He left her standing there with her mouth hanging open in surprise. She watched him depart even as Hawke rushed into the hall from the kitchen.

"I heard we had a visitor. Are you unharmed?" he asked seeing that she was alone.

"Aye… for now."

Her captain watched her closely. "Who is he?"

"Sir Reynard Norwood. He is on a mission for the empress and will sleep in the barn tonight."

"You did not offer him his own bedchamber?"

She turned to face her captain. "Nay but then again, he gave me little choice. He is expecting me to leave here with him."

A curse left Hawke. "That is bold of him."

"Aye. I have the feeling I will not be able to dispatch Sir Reynard so easily. He is… determined."

Hawke silently observed her before he apparently came to his own conclusion. "If we are to look at our situation objectively, now that your grandfather has passed on, the knight might have a point. If we were to travel with his company, you and the few who might agree to accompany us at least would be fed and protected."

Elysande raised her brow at his audacity. "You think it wise to leave Blackmore unattended?"

Hawke shrugged and folded his arms across his massive chest. "What more could anyone who came this way do to the place? There is little left of any value until the land heals. That will take a fair amount of time."

"But Blackmore is my home," she said as her voice hitched with the thought of leaving something she was responsible for and been trying so hard to save."

"Blackmore is just a place, Elysande. It does not define you.

The keep at least still stands and will remain so until your return. I do not think your grandfather would like to watch you from heaven starving to death in your attempts to remain in a place that will not currently serve you, no matter how determined you might be."

A sob caught in her throat and as Hawke stepped forward to most likely offer her some form of comfort, she held up his hand to halt his progress. Before her captain could comment, she whispered she had chores to do and left him there alone. Instead of making her way outside, she instead went to her bedchamber. Her head was suddenly aching, and she could only wonder if Sir Reynard would continue to plague her every waking thought until she could convince him to leave without her.

CHAPTER FIVE

REYNARD HEARD THE barn door open but continued to see to his horse. He assumed Elysande had sought him out after coming to the conclusion there was nothing left for her here. At least for now. He did not expect a knight with blond hair to come within his vision. He finished what he was doing and closed the stall door. He was wary of the man before him but Reynard did not feel as though he needed to draw his sword.

"I see the lady is not alone after all. Who are you?" he asked leaning back against the wooden wall of the stall.

"'Tis I who should be asking who *you* are, sir. Do you think you can just arrive here and expect the lady to leave her home with a total stranger?" the man growled out with a soft accent.

Reynard nodded. "I see the lady has at least filled you in on my plans for her to travel with us."

"Us?"

"Aye. The knights I travel with for the empress should be arriving shortly. We head to Bristol then onward to Winchester."

"Who are you?" the knight asked again.

"Sir Reynard Norwood. One of several men who have given their loyalty to the Empress Matilda." Reynard waited for the man to also inform him who he was, especially to the lady.

"Sir Hawke de Challon. Captain of the Guard to Lady Elysande Thorburn of Blackmore."

"Blackmore does not appear to have much left of a garrison. Are you all that remains?" Reynard inquired whilst his gaze swept the entrance to the barn as if expecting more knights to suddenly fill the empty space.

"Aye, and a handful of servants. Stephen's men took care of the rest by either killing them or unwillingly enlisting those who yet lived. 'Twas not a pretty sight and with her grandfather passing and her parents abroad, Lady Elysande has been through much on her own."

"All the more reason for her to travel with us. She will be well protected."

"You assume much, sir. What makes you think you can take control over her?" Hawke asked with a raised brow. "Trust me when I tell you, Lady Elysande is perfectly capable of taking care of herself."

Reynard smirked. "Aye, so she told me, but in all honesty, how will you all survive the coming winter? I am concerned that if I leave her behind, she will starve herself trying to see to those she is still responsible for. If she were to leave with us, then her people are more than welcome to also travel with the empress's army or return to their kin."

"I attempted to make a point of suggesting that leaving with you might be beneficial to all those concerned. She is still determined to see to the needs of those who have remained loyal to her," Hawke said with a heavy sigh, "at any cost."

"Starving herself to death to feed the others will prove nothing." Reynard folded his arms over his chest. "Surely, you as her captain and who must know her best, can reach out to her so she might see clearly how dire her situation has become."

"I have tried. She is… stubborn to say the least."

A short laugh escaped Reynard. "Then I will continue to plead my case and will attempt to change her mind. 'Tis in her best interest, after all."

"In your opinion…"

"Aye. I cannot in good conscience leave a woman alone when 'tis clear she cannot survive for much longer considering the condition of her lands." The sound of horses arriving outside caused Reynard to halt his conversation before continuing. "That will be the arrival of the empress's men."

The two knights left the stable and Reynard went to the lead horseman. "Richard," he called out, "your arrival is most timely."

Richard scanned the area. "Timely? We appear to be too late to be of much use here. Who is this?"

Reynard made the necessary introductions. "There is a problem," he began.

"We do not have time for problems, Reynard, as you very well know. We cannot dally when we are about the empress's business," Richard declared resting one arm on the pommel of his saddle.

"There is a lady—"

"—when is there not, of late," Richard laughed. "They seem to be plaguing us no matter what we might say about not needing them in our lives."

Reynard grimaced. "Even so, I have made a vow to her and offered her my protection."

Richard nodded toward Hawke. "She has a captain to protect her. She does not need *you*."

Hawke chuckled and gave Reynard a smug *I told you so* look.

Reynard stood taller. "The vow has been made and I will not recant my words. As you can see for yourself, there is not much left here for her to survive."

"'Tis none of our concern," Richard muttered. "Get your horse and let us away. We can be in Bristol within the hour."

"I cannot. Surely you understand a knight's vow. My honor is at stake."

"You create havoc wherever you may go of late, Reynard. You think nothing of your previous vow to our empress and think only of another pretty woman who has barely crossed your path," Richard reminded him.

"The empress will understand. As soon as I convince the lady to travel with us, I can catch up to you at Bristol," Reynard said crossing his arms again over his chest. He was determined to see that Elysande be kept safe and fed.

"'Tis your neck if the empress learns that you did not adhere to her directives." Richard sat up once more in his saddle. "Catch up within the next day or two. I will not wait for you and the lady before I move the men onward toward Winchester."

Before he left, he called out to one of the other men who brought forth several birds and tossed them at Reynard's feet. If nothing else, they would eat well this night. He would worry about the morrow when the time came.

CHAPTER SIX

AFTER A BRIEF rest in her room, Elysande had collected her composure and began to go about her daily chores. She had never been one to hide away in her room when trouble crossed her path. Now would be no different despite the man who would be sleeping in her barn.

The ruckus of multiple horses arriving in her bailey had momentarily alarmed her and when she opened the shutters and gazed out of her window, she could see Reynard below talking with the men. She had breathed a sigh of relief that the keep was not again under attack. She should not have worried anyway. There was not much left for anyone to take.

She thought of the few coins and jewelry she had stashed away in her father's solar prior to the siege. A lose brick in the wall had been the perfect place to hide what little valuables were left. Unless you knew where to look, no one would espy it. She thought everything would remain safe after the barbican gate had been breached. Unfortunately, such had not been the case. The thieving horde who had ransacked her home had discovered the last bit of wealth she had saved along with her small horde of treasures. They had laughed as they'd collected everything of value and left her with nothing to sell to see to her people's needs.

Now she was once more vexed with a handsome knight who turned up everywhere she went this day. *Handsome! By Saint Michael's Wings!* Why did such a thought sweep across her mind?

'Twas those steel grey eyes of his that felt as though they were attempting to burrow their way into her soul. She would not fall under his spell. He only wished for her to comply to his demands. There was no way he would sway her. No way she would leave Blackmore with a complete stranger.

Still… he was becoming annoying and trying what little she had left of her patience. Sir Reynard turned up first just outside of her bedchamber door. How he knew which room belonged to her was beyond her kin. But there he had stood… one booted foot propped against the stone wall. His arms had been folded across that muscled chest, and he wore a smirk as though he knew he would eventually win his point by wearing her down. He had asked if she was packed, and she muttered a curse leaving him behind whilst making her way to the turret.

She made it without his presence through one chore of advising the few servants in the kitchen to prepare porridge until she learned that several birds had been provided for their evening meal. She was thankful for they would have more than what she could have provided when it came time to sup.

But her solitude was again interrupted when she went to the garden to dig in the ground for several vegetables. This time he sat on a stone bench and watched her intently. One leg was crossed over the other until he again asked if she was ready to depart. She had murmured something to the effect that he could help with finding what was left in her garden to go with their meal. He laughed and left her there to her own devices, the ungallant bastard. Did he think their food would just magically appear for his dining pleasure?

The barn was next when she went to milk the cow. Leaning on one of the posts as if he did not have a care in the world, his smile would have caused most women to swoon, she supposed. Luckily, she was not one of those women. Once the pail was full, she had left the stall and motioned for him to take the bucket. One dark brow had risen as if to mock her. He then proceeded to tell her the only thing he would lift was her satchel of clothes so they could depart. So much for chivalry and helping a lady in need.

Now, he followed behind her as she carefully carried the pail of milk in an attempt to not spill the container. They passed what was left of her smithy, where Hawke was busy sharpening several blades. She continued onward, eager to rid herself of the man who followed her. But he would not be so easily dismissed as he began whistling a merry tune. She had had enough and turned to face the cad.

"Do you not have something better to do?" she asked tartly, setting down the bucket whilst she addressed this frustrating knight.

"Nay, although you must know that we are wasting valuable time. I have places to go and must not tarry here long," he declared before he ran a hand through his dark tresses. Several strands stood on end, and she tried not to chuckle at the sight of him looking like the rooster in her chicken coop.

"Do not let me keep you, Sir Knight. There is no reason to delay your departure." She picked up her pail and began once again making her way toward the rear entry to the keep. She called back over her shoulder. "Godspeed to you."

He caught up with her and at last took the bucket from her hands. She took a sideways glance at him but remained silent until they entered the kitchen, and he finally found his voice.

"You know I cannot leave you behind knowing your situation here at Blackmore is dire, my lady. When will you see reason?" he asked until he went to sit on a stool at the large wooden table in the center of the room.

"Never," she replied before pushing several vegetables and a knife in his direction. "Be useful and cut these."

He took up the knife and began cutting the carrots, turnips, and onions into cubes. "Never is a long time, Elysande. You shall starve yourself and those who remain with you, or have you not thought that far ahead?"

She turned her back to him and heaved a sigh. *Of course, she had thought of that,* she fumed. Every. Single. Day! Composing herself once more she turned to face the man invading her kitchen. "You are so annoying," she snapped in irritation that she could not make this man go away.

His laughter filled the room. "You are not the first to inform me of such a trait and you certainly will not be the last. But surely you can see my point. Close up the keep until your return or for when your parents travel back home. You will be safer with me and those who are about the empress's business."

"And who will keep me safe from the advances of those same men in your company? You?" she inquired and then blushed that she had spoken her thoughts aloud.

He set down the knife. "I offered you my protection. My vow still stands. I am fully aware you do not know me or my nature but I am hardly in the habit of accosting women to see my needs fulfilled—"

A gasp escaped her that they were having such a conversation. "I did not say that you and I—" She bit her lips shut when he raised his hand to halt whatever words would spill forth next from her mouth.

"—nor do I take that which is not *freely* offered," he finished with a sly grin waiting for that answer to sink into her muddled brain.

"I am offering you nothing but a place to rest your head… alone."

A chuckle escaped his lips. "A pity." He took up the knife and continued the task she had given him. "If you feel so uncomfortable traveling with strangers, then by all means bring your captain and maid and anyone else you would like. I care not who you wish to travel with so long as we make haste. I offer them the same protection that I offer you. If whoever you choose to ride with can keep up with the pace of our army, then there will be no problem. We wait for no one who cannot travel at the speed needed to meet our objectives."

She was surprised at his words. "You have given me much to

think on," she murmured softly.

"Do not take too long to mull over your decision. I would much rather have you come willingly than for me to take you by force because you are too stubborn to see this as a remedy to your situation and is for your own good."

She narrowed her eyes at this man's gall. Just when she thought she might consider his offer, he goes and ruins it all. "You would not dare!" Hands on hips, she stomped her foot to get her point across only causing Reynard to give her a sly grin.

"Try me…"

With that challenge tossed in her direction and his task complete, he stood. Giving her a short bow of his head, he left her there sputtering and cursing his name. She swore she could hear his laughter echoing in the great hall. *Bloody hell!* He was going to make her leave whether she wished it or not. She hated him!

When the rear door opened again, Elysande briefly closed her eyes to give herself strength, gritted her teeth, and took a deep breath to confront the man who had returned to attempt again to persuade her to leave Blackmore. She turned to face the scoundrel and sighed in relief when she espied Hawke entering the kitchen.

He sat down at the bench, took up the knife, and continued to cut the vegetables still waiting on the table. "You appeared flustered when I saw you walking with Sir Reynard. Are you all right?"

"He vexes me," she muttered trying to come to terms with leaving. She sat down next to her captain who inspected her intently. "Go on… out with it."

"Out with what?" he said barely containing the slight smirk to his lips.

"Do not play games with me, Hawke. Tell me your thoughts so we may get this conversation over with. I am not certain I can bear further soul searching for one day," she stated, folding her hands in her lap. She clenched her fingertips together, ready for whatever would spill forth from the man whose council she most trusted.

"As I have already stated, my lady, you and I both know that Sir Reynard speaks the truth. Whilst there are not many of us left here at Blackmore, there are still too many to feed with the limited sources we have available. You would do well to heed Sir Reynard's words so that we may travel with him to the empress." Hawke finished his task and tossed the vegetables into a cast iron pot on the table.

Elysande raised her tortured blue eyes to face him. "You would come with me?"

He gave her a smile. "To the ends of the earth if need be."

'Twas as though a heavy burden were suddenly lifted from her shoulders, just from knowing her faithful captain would agree to travel with her. "Mayhap we could quickly make arrangements for the remaining servants to return to their families. They have been devoted to me, and I will not see them remain here and starve," she replied finally coming to terms with her situation.

Hawke nodded. "I am certain we can make such an arrangement—and I am glad you came to the conclusion to leave Blackmore of your own accord."

A snort left her. "'Twas hardly of my own accord, Hawke, and you know it."

"Aye… well… mayhap Sir Reynard had a little something to do with your decision."

Elysande reached over and clasped Hawke's hand. His eyes momentarily widened at her touch. She almost regretted showing this warrior this small bit of affection until she felt him gently squeeze her hand.

"Thank you for standing by me all this time, Hawke." How could she adequately express her gratitude to this man? There were not enough words to convey how highly she valued all he had done for her both before and after the siege.

Hawke stood and gave her a bow. "I am forever your most humble servant, my lady. I had best see to what can be done for the other servants prior to our leaving and see to packing."

Elysande watched him leave. When more servants came into the kitchen, she gave the task of preparing the evening meal over to others. She went to stand at the entrance to her great hall and her eyes swept the room as memories flooded her mind. There really was no other choice but to go, and yet she hated to leave this place. More importantly, she would hate to see the smug look of satisfaction plastered on Sir Reynard's face when he realized he had convinced her to leave. She swore she would hate him for all time!

CHAPTER SEVEN

R EYNARD'S GAZE TRAVELED over his shoulder to view the woman who had reluctantly come around to his way of thinking. She appeared miserable and he supposed he could not blame her. She must have felt his stare for her head jerked upright, her brows narrowed, and then she stuck her tongue out before turning away with a look of what appeared disgust. A childish act but so be it. Hate him if she must, but Reynard still felt he had made the right decision to bring her with him.

He had thought that by turning up wherever she went would eventually wear down the walls she had erected around her. They were bound to tumble just as surely as the stones surrounding her keep. She had not made his task of getting her to change her mind easy, but he had been as determined as she was. After all... how could he in good conscience leave a woman behind when she could barely feed herself let alone the few servants who remained loyal to her household?

It had taken her two long days of sulking before she sent Hawke to deliver her decision. Two long days of making her so angry with him that he swore she would drive a knife into his chest if given half a chance. Aye... she hated him with every breath she took but at least she would be safe.

The memory of when she turned the key into the lock of the front door of her keep would most likely haunt him for years to come. His own memories had briefly flashed before his eyes. At times, it felt as if 'twas just yesterday when he and his brothers had been forced to flee Brockenhurst. Once the key had been put away, Elysande had rested her forehead and one hand on the solid wooden portal as though she was saying a final farewell to the place. But 'twas the tormented look in her tear-filled blue eyes that would have been any man's downfall. Reynard almost reconsidered… almost. But he hardened his heart, took up the reins of his horse, and waited whilst her captain assisted her into the saddle. He could feel her stare boring into his back ever since.

"She will come around, Sir Reynard," Hawke said as if reading his thoughts. "She may be stubborn, but she eventually saw reason and came to her own conclusion that we were right."

"She was acting childish and thinking only of herself," Reynard retorted whilst keeping alert for possible attacks upon the open road.

A sound rumbled in the chest of Elysande's captain. "I suppose that is what you would see not knowing her as I do. She is only a score of years. Even though she is young, Lady Elysande has had the responsibility of her people thrust upon her when her parents went to travel abroad for their own entertainment for the past five years. 'Twas not easy caring for a dying grandfather and watching a man she adored slip away from this world. Give her a chance to come to terms with her new life. She will not disappoint you."

Reynard's brow rose. "Disappoint me?" he queried. "I have no feelings for your mistress so she cannot in truth disappoint me. My one and only concern was her welfare. Once we are again in the presence of the empress, I will leave the lady in our monarch's care."

Hawke leveled his gaze upon Reynard and then frowned before turning his attention once more upon the road ahead of them. "I thought mayhap since you were so adamant upon her leaving Blackmore, that you had quickly developed an affection for her."

"I barely know the woman," Reynard scoffed. The thought of falling under some woman's spell was more than abhorrent to him. He had made himself a vow never to fall in love again. He had every notion to keep the promise he had made in his youth, did he not?

"She would make some man an excellent wife," the Frenchman replied quietly. "She has been well trained in all that would be required of her once she married."

"Then *you* wed her," Reynard retorted. "I assure you I have no plans to wed her or any other woman."

"Never? That seems odd considering all men would eventually take a wife to fill their coffers and ensure their line continues," Hawke said, taking a short glance at the lady riding behind them.

Reynard cursed beneath his breath reminding himself once again of the vow he had sworn to himself in his youth never to marry. Inwardly, he sighed knowing 'twas foolish and one he knew some day he would unwillingly need to break. If nothing else, the empress would choose a bride for him with lands to further her claim to England. "I have no plans to marry anytime *soon*," Reynard said rephrasing his reply from moments ago. "I am in service to the empress and am not at liberty to do as I please. But if the lady is so worthy to marry, again I have to ask, why do you not wed with her?"

"She has been under my protection since she was a little child," he said with a slight smile. "Her elevated status of a noble house made such a union impossible anyway. Her parents would have never approved. Besides, Lady Elysande is more like a sister to me and I could not think of her otherwise."

Reynard nodded. "I understand. My brothers and I have a woman who has been a friend of the family for most of our lives. She developed an affection for my older brother Wymar but he, too, would never cross the boundaries of falling for his best friend's sister."

"You have brothers," Hawke mentioned.

"Aye, two older, both now wed. I have been traveling with that same friend Lord Richard Grancourt and several others whom I fought beside at Lincoln and Winchester."

"You were at both battles and survived. Rumor has it there was not much left to Winchester once the bishop lit fire to the place."

"Aye. We were lucky to escape capture when we fled with the empress. 'Twill take years for Winchester to recover from the fires."

Hawke nodded. "And Lady Elysande... you will just leave her in the care of our monarch and return to whatever tasks the empress has in mind for you?"

"'Tis my way of life. I am duty bound to Empress Matilda until she releases me from her service. I am certain Lady Elysande will find plenty of prospects for her hand at court."

Hawke's brow rose. "Lady Elysande is not accustomed to court life. I have the feeling she will hate the intrigues that surround such a life more than she currently hates you," he grumbled. "But obviously I was wrong about my assumption earlier and misspoke about you possibly finding you may one day hold an affection for the lady. I apologize and will not bring the matter up again."

Hawke pulled on the reins of his horse and fell back into place next to his lady, leaving Reynard alone with his thoughts. Another glance at the woman in question and his head began to ache since she reminded him so much of Lady Johanna. Nay! He would not fall under Elysande's spell no matter how beautiful the lady might be. He continued that mantra inside his head until he almost believed his own thoughts. He wondered how many times he would need to repeat them until they stuck.

CHAPTER EIGHT

ELYSANDE PULLED ON the reins of her horse to halt its progress once she reached the inner bailey of Bristol Castle. She raised her head to stare up at the towering keep and could only wonder what awaited her inside. Her emotions had been a jumbled mess since locking Blackmore's door this morn. She had left everything behind of her old life and had left a note for whenever her parents might return. She had bid farewell to the few remaining servants after Hawke made arrangements for their own travel, reiterating to them that she would one day return to Blackmore with the hope they, too, might wish to return to serve her household when that time came.

She was thankful that Hawke remained by her side. Her maid Olive had also been a pleasant surprise when she refused to leave her mistress. But they were all that was left of the life she had known. Her world had been turned upside down by a pair of steel grey eyes.

Her own watched Reynard whilst he was welcomed by several knights, one of whom she recognized from when he had ordered food be brought forward for their meal whilst still at Blackmore. The camaraderie between the two knights was unquestionable and 'twas clear these men were friends beyond their service to their empress. Several laughed at what one of them had said, causing Reynard to scowl. Whatever comment had been mentioned was directed at the younger knight.

Elysande had had plenty of time to study Reynard whilst they traveled the short distance to Bristol. Though he could not be much older than she herself was, at times she felt much younger in comparison. Mayhap 'twas because of the battles he had fought that made him seem older than his years. Or perchance she considered herself younger because she had always been tied to the responsibilities of caring for Blackmore and its people, which meant that she never had the chance to see much of the world. Whatever the reason, Elysande had tried to keep her demeaner indifferent to the man she had sworn to hate. Yet, whenever his gaze turned in her direction, her heart betrayed her and flipped end over end. She swore she would not fall under his spell.

Reynard pointed in her direction. Hawke and Olive sat upon their own horses slightly behind her. She turned her head and whispered Hawke's name. He pressed his steed forward until his horse came parallel with her own.

"Are we safe here?" she asked lifting her eyes to meet her captain's.

"We are probably safer here with these knights then left to our own devices back at Blackmore," he stated before taking off his leather gloves and tucking them into the belt at his waist. "At least we have the protection of many instead of trying to do everything with the few servants we had left. Without your guardsmen, we were left vulnerable."

"I can only pray that they will return to Blackmore once we are finally allowed to make our way home—and that when that time comes, things will look differently from how they were when we left the place. I felt horrible releasing the servants from their service to my family," she murmured.

"They understood your dire circumstances, my lady, and took no offense. They were lucky they yet lived after Stephen's army got through with the place," Hawke answered with his soft French accent that used to cause her heart to soar in her youth. Now he was more like the older brother that she'd never had.

Elysande nodded. "I still do not like the fact that Sir Reynard forced my hand," she hissed, and her eyes drifted back to the man who continued to creep into her head at all hours of the day. Nay, 'twas worse than that, for not only had he physically shown up wherever she went at Blackmore, but he had also unknowingly invaded her dreams at night. A rosy blush flushed her face whilst she remembered some of those visions. They had been so intimate. So vivid, filled with a passion she had never experienced before in all her score of years. They had embedded themselves in her mind so completely that at times she swore she could almost still feel his touch upon her bare skin. 'Twas as if her mind betrayed how she really felt about a knight she barely knew but yearned to know in every aspect. *God's Bones*!

"I was pleased you came to the decision to leave. There was nothing left for us at Blackmore, and you know it, Elysande," Hawke replied, using her given name to add extra weight to his words.

She frowned and watched whilst Reynard left his friends and began making his way back in her direction. She nodded to Hawke. "See to Olive and ensure she is settled for the night. My guess is we will not linger long here at Bristol."

Hawke's eyes narrowed watching Reynard's steady approach. "Are you certain you do not wish for me to stay by your side, my lady?"

"Aye." She did not say another word. If anything, Elysande knew she would be safe with so many around if she had to call for aid. Besides, with her still sitting on her horse, she had the upper hand and the height to feel dominant over the man who stood upon the ground.

"Let me assist you from your horse, my lady," Reynard said, holding up his hands.

A sly smirk crept across her lips. "I am more than capable of dismounting myself, sir," she said watching as his brow furrowed.

"Do you plan to hate me all the way to Oxford?" he asked settling his arms across that well-muscled chest.

She could not help the light laugh that escaped her mouth, even when it caused the line of Reynard's own mouth to creep ever so slightly upward. "Mayhap. Time will tell, Sir Knight."

A chuckle rumbled in his chest. "Well then… until you figure out how you shall treat me on a day-to-day basis, why do you not give me this one concession by allowing my chivalrous nature to speak for itself by helping you?"

"I still hate you for making me leave my home." She took off her leather gloves and wondered if she should just jump down from her horse to spite him.

"I understand completely," he replied, staring up at her.

"Such an emotion most likely will continue for some time to come," she continued whilst swinging one leg over the pommel of her saddle. She was still unaccustomed to wearing a tunic and hose, but Hawke and Reynard had suggested she would be more comfortable in a man's attire than traveling wearing a gown that would not permit her to sit astride in the saddle.

"I will not even make an attempt to change your mind in regard to me," Reynard attested, stepping forward and once more holding up his hands. "May I?"

"Aye. I suppose," she at last said, leaning down to rest her palms on his shoulders.

She tried not to think of him holding her close when her body slid down the front of his chest. Nor when their eyes met and held upon her descent to the ground. Nay! Her fingers continued to feel the fabric of his tunic until she remembered herself. Tilting her head back, she felt so small standing next to this tall warrior, and she gulped when the pounding of her heart once again betrayed her tangled feelings.

Another chuckle left him as though he knew the direction in which her thoughts had strayed. Instead of making some snide comment, he instead took hold of her hand and tucked it into the crook of his elbow. "Let me introduce you to my friends. They will treat you with the utmost respect and I know that they, too, shall watch over and protect you."

She could only nod her reply. When he took her the short distance to where the men waited, Elysande did her best to remember their names. Richard, Blake, Kingsley and Oswin all bowed before her as they were each presented to her. All handsome rogues whom Elysande would need to protect her heart from or else it would surely be lost to one of these knights.

CHAPTER NINE

REYNARD SAT AT a long table in the great hall eating his meal. Those closest to him sat at the same table with Elysande and her captain at the far end. She was far enough away that she would not be able to hear their hushed conversations unless they wished to make them audible by raising their voices to include her. But still… she was close enough that he could still watch over her, not that Hawke wasn't capable of such a deed. Reynard frowned, confused by his own protectiveness. Why he was bothering worrying over the woman when she was certainly protected by a knight who had been performing such a duty for many a year? The lady did not need him, and he could only ponder his stupidity for making such a vow.

But the deed was done, and Reynard now felt obligated to carry out his words. Whilst joining the rest of the team that would head to Winchester come the morn, Elysande would barely come within arms distance to him, or so he presumed. But that was of little import. There were enough knights here to ensure her safety as they traveled. He would not need to be directly involved.

Her laughter rang out and drew the knights nearby to gaze upon her as if they were moths flying into a flame. The sound was infectious, causing Reynard to steel his heart against falling under her spell. Aye… she was casting her magic toward every male around her whether she knew it or not. Reynard could already see for himself that Kingsley hung onto her every word.

He was certain 'twould not be long before Blake did the same if his cow-eyed attention to the woman was any indication as to where his feelings could lie.

Richard gave him a nudge, and Reynard turned his attention back to the man seated next to him.

"You did not hear a word I said," Richard stated with a frown. "'Tis clear you have been besotted with the young lady since we caught up with you at Blackmore. Get your head out of the clouds and pay attention."

"I am *not* besotted," Reynard grumbled before taking his eyes from the black-haired beauty sitting at the far end of the table.

"Aye, you are, *mon ami*. You do not have the time to indulge in a frivolous affair with the lady. We already accommodated you for the extra days you spent convincing her to leave her home. We must needs leave for Winchester come the morn. Even now, we are two days behind schedule." Richard took a sip from his chalice, but his worried frown never left his brow.

"Have no fear, Richard. There are no plans hatching inside my head to have an affair with Lady Elysande now or in my future. She is only under my protection until I can deliver her into the empress's keeping," Reynard replied taking a drink of his wine.

"I was concerned. She is almost too similar in her features to that of Lady Johanna. The lady from Blackmore could be your lady reincarnated."

Reynard almost choked on his wine as he set the chalice down. "You see it, too?" he asked in a hushed whisper. This alone was reason enough for Reynard to stay as far away from Elysande as humanly possible.

"'Tis hard to miss the resemblance since I also knew of your affection for the young lady in your youth. I know how much Lady Johanna's death left its mark on you," Richard said pointing a two-pronged fork at Reynard. "But you need to think clearly for whatever may await us in Winchester. Do not lose your head to a pretty face and a shapely body."

Reynard glanced momentarily at Elysande before returning his attention to his meal. "You expect trouble upon our arrival at Winchester?" he asked not taking the bait to comment on the Lady Elysande's beauty. Anyone with half a mind could see for himself the woman was indeed attractive.

"'Tis hard to say. I would like the prisoner exchange to be peaceful, but one never knows what to expect where King Stephen is concerned. Let us pray that we can hand him over and in return take the earl and escape with our heads still attached."

"The sooner we leave Winchester the better. I cannot imagine there is much left to the town after the bishop finished setting fire to the place," Reynard dryly commented.

With their conversation done, he ate his meal in silence. His mood plunged with each bit of laughter that rang out from the other end of the table. Obviously, the men were enthralled with their conversation with the lady who continued to keep them entertained. But as the hall began to empty when the hour grew late, Reynard stayed where he was until Elysande stifled a yawn. She apologized to those around her and finally stood, causing Reynard to do the same. He could not miss the glance she gave him before she began bidding each man a good night.

When the lady came to stand next to him after dismissing her captain, Reynard was not sure if he was surprised or mayhap a bit mystified. He was about to ask how he might be of service when she spoke her thoughts.

"Will you walk with me, Sir Reynard?" she asked in a breathy whisper. She placed her hand in the crook of his elbow giving him no chance to decline.

"Where would you have me escort you, my lady?" he asked as curiosity got the better of him.

"Perchance a quick walk outside in the garden before retiring for the eve?" she suggested. "I understand the night is not too cool so we may enjoy a short stroll."

He nodded his acceptance of her idea and led her out the keep door. A short while later, they were strolling in the moonlit garden area. The path was neat and pleasant enough, although the flowers had all but died for the season.

"Is there a reason you asked me to accompany you instead of your captain?" he asked breaking the silence that stretched between them.

"My conversation with Hawke earlier had me thinking I was mayhap too harsh in my assessment of you." Her fingertips traced his arm, and he was certain she was not aware that she was causing his skin to tingle from her touch.

He cleared his throat, taking a moment to get his thoughts in order. "I thought your plan was to hate me," he responded with a slight chuckle. They came to a stone bench, and she went to take a seat, motioning toward him to do the same. This brought him far closer to the woman than he would have wished. Aye... she was weaving some sort of spell around him, and he was unaware how to get out of this situation without losing his head.

"As I said... mayhap I was overreacting just a bit." The smile she gave him was that of an innocent, and he was certain that if he could see her in the light of day, a rosy blush would be rushing across her cheeks.

"In the end, you came to see reason on how dire your situation was, so how you think of me hardly matters," he said quickly. She reached over to take his hand causing his eyes to widen at the contact.

"Mayhap we can start anew?" she asked. Those blue eyes held such promise... but Reynard could in no way give her hope that they had a future together.

"Elysande—"

"—and perchance you will forgive me for this..."

He was completely unprepared when she quickly leaned forward to place her lips upon his own. 'Twas a chaste kiss and showed Reynard how inexperienced this young lady truly was. He should have stood and escorted her back into the keep and up to her bedchamber. He should have told her they had no future together. But as a part of him rose to prove to Reynard just how attractive he honestly found the lady, he could not help himself from leaning forward to kiss her once again.

$$\cdot \;\text{❦}\; \cdot$$

CHAPTER TEN

E LYSANDE MUST HAVE lost her mind when she started this mild
flirtation with Reynard. She had watched him intently
during the evening meal and saw for herself the subtle looks of
appreciation he gave her when he did not think she would see.
Perchance she was imagining the whole exchange but a part of
her soul that craved the adventure she'd never had the luxury to
indulge in called to her to explore what might happen with this
handsome knight. Aye… she could not deny the attraction she
felt for the man, no matter how she vowed to hate him.

Mayhap she should blame the wine she had drunk this eve.
She had only wanted to apologize to this man for her earlier
behavior. But between the moonlight and watching him this eve,
'twas as though some force had pushed her forward to press her
lips to Reynard's. She was almost embarrassed of the childish
peck on his mouth that proved she had no knowledge of how this
kissing business was supposed to occur between a man and a
woman. But how quickly the situation changed once Reynard
leaned forward and slid his lips along her own.

His tongue followed along the seam of her mouth causing her
to gasp whilst heat rushed throughout her body. But apparently
this was the response he wanted for his tongue slipped forward
and began to tangle with her own. A moan escaped her from the
deepest depths of her soul. Her arms wound their way over his
broad shoulders and her fingers began twining themselves in his
dark brown hair. She was lost… or mayhap she was found, and

she surrendered herself to the sensations this man was sharing with her. Aye, he was teaching her what he liked when he deepened their kiss and she completely forgot everything else but Reynard. From the low moan that rumbled in his chest, Elysande was thrilled to note that Reynard was also enjoying this moment they took for themselves.

A name rushed from his mouth when he began trailing kisses down her cheek to her neck. His hand tightened around her waist pulling her forward until they were chest to chest. Her heart beat a rapid staccato that *nearly* drowned out everything else—but then the reality of what he had whispered in the heat of the moment finally penetrated her brain.

She broke off the kiss and pushed upon that rock-hard chest to put some distance between them. His eyes may be passion filled but he clearly had been thinking of another.

"Who is Johanna?" she demanded as soon as she found her voice. She stood, quickly straightening her gown and patting down her disheveled hair.

"What?" Reynard asked in confusion. His brows furrowed and he held out his hand as if she would take it after that.

"Johanna. Who is she?" Elysande asked again.

"No one," he answered in a firm tone as he, too, came to his feet.

"Well, she is obviously someone since you thought of her whilst kissing me." She shook her head in a ridiculous attempt to clear it so she could regain her sanity. What a fool she had been! To think that mayhap something could blossom between this man and her.

"Elysande, let me explain," Reynard said stepping forward.

She stepped back and held out her hand to halt his progress forward. "Nay. 'Twas a foolish notion to begin with. I should have never initiated a kiss between us. I promise you I will not push myself on you again. You can go live your life with your fair Johanna."

"Elysande, please..." he began but she wanted nothing further to do with Sir Reynard Norwood.

She whirled around to find her way out of the garden only to have her arm grabbed when Reynard took hold of her trembling limb. "Release me!" she ordered, and he immediately let go of her.

"I am sorry," Reynard said with what appeared as honest regret. "I should have never kissed you, let alone taken things as far as I did. I cannot offer you the life you deserve," he replied in what sounded like a sincere heart… not that it mattered. What did she care if he whispered another woman's name whilst his lips were upon her own?

"Did I ask you for a life together?" she declared sharply. "'Twas only a simple kiss."

One dark brow above his eyes lifted. "To some women, there is nothing simple about a kiss between two people."

A sarcastic sound escaped her as she made every attempt to once more guard her heart. "Then you should be thankful that I am *not* one of those women."

"You are not?" he asked as though he did not believe her words.

He was correct not to believe her for if anything, the kiss between her and this man had left her completely rattled and defenseless. "Nay, I am not," she lied. She lifted her chin defiantly as though doing so would prove her words held a ring of truth.

Reynard peered at her in the moonlight. "Then this was nothing more than a flirtatious gesture on your part, much like you gathered the attention of the knights around you whilst you supped?" He folded his arms across his chest waiting for her answer. She could see for herself how agitated he was if his clenched jaw was any indication of his current mood.

"What more could it be?" The words rushed from her lips even as she saw the frown appear on his brow.

"I did not take you for one of those women who are so driven with their frivolous nature that they seek only to gain the attention of men around her."

She snapped her mouth shut whilst she pondered her reply. Frivolous? She was far from such a judge of her character considering this attempt at giving a man any form of her affection had been her first try. She had been the first one to moan in pleasure at their kiss. He, on the other hand, had then whispered another's name. If his own affections lay elsewhere, with this Johanna, then was he not the frivolous one for kissing her with such intensity?

"You barely know me, Reynard, so how could you know what or who I am?" she replied although once her words left her lips, she regretted them. But the deed was done and now this knight would only think the worst of her.

A sound of discontent seemingly rumbled inside his chest before he looked down at her. "And to think Hawke thought you would not fit in well at court," he sneered before he once more composed himself. "You will, indeed, fit in very well with all their intrigues and affairs that will hold no commitment to those involved."

"I look forward to the experience and to attending our empress," she answered as she continued to hold his gaze.

"I will see you to your bedchamber," Reynard stated, holding out his arm.

A snort left her. "You do not have to bother, Sir Reynard. I leave you to your own devices and to dream of being reunited with your fair Johanna."

She abruptly left him whilst his cursing echoed in the air behind her. She quickened her pace when his footsteps hastened to follow her. She began to run as fast as her feet would carry her. Once she gained entrance to her chamber, she slid the bolt home even as tears of loneliness slid down her cheeks. Whatever brief thoughts she had of exploring any kind of intimacy with Reynard was at an end. His heart belonged to someone else.

CHAPTER ELEVEN

November 2, 1141

REYNARD KEPT HIS gaze focused on the road ahead of him as he rode his horse in the direction of Winchester. They had close to one hundred miles to travel and had begun their journey the day before. He refused to give the woman he had dreamed about last eve the least bit of his attention. She could flirt her way through the entire court for all he cared. After all, she had already started by gaining the attention of his friends. Her laughter rang out in the afternoon air as they reached the outskirts of Winchester, causing Reynard to grind his teeth together in frustration.

He knew his duties to his empress needed to be at the forefront of his mind. The exchange of King Stephen for the empress's half-brother Earl Robert was of the utmost of importance. This was all he needed to concentrate on. This was his main concern. The exchange of the prisoners had been previously organized and the condition for each man's release was simple. Both men did not have to swear to anything and were free to resume their positions and defend the party they had pledged themselves to prior to being taken.

But the actual arrangements for the exchange were far more complex considering neither party trusted one another. 'Twas arranged that when King Stephen left Bristol Castle, his queen, Matilda, one of his sons, and also two magnates of high rank would be left at the castle under close guard. Upon the exchange in Winchester, Earl Robert would then leave behind his eldest son and heir William. Once Robert returned to Bristol, Queen Matilda and the rest would be released. They would then return to Winchester where Robert's son would also gain his freedom. What could possibly go wrong?

Everything could go wrong between the two locations, including losing whatever sanity Reynard had left inside him. Whispering Johanna's name whilst kissing Elysande had been a huge mistake on his part. He should have made the lady listen to his explanation that Johanna had passed away but when Elysande admitted that kissing him meant nothing to her, Reynard felt like the biggest fool in all of Christendom! Aye, he had let a pretty face and those blue eyes take him under her spell and mayhap that had been his first mistake. He swore he was never going to do so again.

An amused chuckle rumbled in the chest of the man who rode next to him. "You have fallen out with the fair lady, it appears," Richard teased, casting a glance at Reynard. "You will not pursue her?"

"There is nothing between Lady Elysande and myself," Reynard grumbled. "I have more important matters to pay attention to than some female who flirts with anyone within her reach."

Richard frowned. "Funny… I do not see her in such a light. She is young, perhaps, but certainly not careless in her affections."

A grunt left Reynard. "What does it matter? She can do as she pleases. Let some other knight deal with her behavior. I could not care less where her affections might lie."

"'Tis good that you put your head back into your duties to our empress. For a few moments, I thought we lost you much as we lost your two brothers who now both enjoy marital bliss."

"Bah! I have no time to be saddled with a woman nor to take responsibility for her. Let Lady Elysande find herself a husband amongst these knights or with the lords at court. As long as I am not within her reach, I will feel lucky."

"Then mayhap you should not look so fierce whenever you decide to look upon the lovely lady, *mon ami*," Richard declared with another laugh. "Your visage betrays your true feelings for the woman. You had best learn to hide them or all will know you care for her."

Richard gave Reynard no time to reply as he kicked his heel into his steed's side and trotted up ahead where King Stephen was under heavy guard. Reynard let Richard's words sink into his head. He had no idea that his face betrayed his true feelings for Elysande. He would admit, if only to himself, that he found her attractive but mayhap that was only due to the close resemblance to Johanna. In either case, he in truth did not have time to dally with a woman. That had not changed from the moment he first came upon her weeping in the graveyard.

As they reached what was left of the town of Winchester, Reynard's gaze traveled to the burned-out buildings, the walls in need of repair, and the downtrodden condition of the people they passed. With time all could be repaired, but at the moment, there wasn't much left of the city. It seemed like it was just yesterday that he had fled this place with his empress, and the difference in it from then to now was stark and unsettling. As he continued forward he could see for himself that the town had begun its repairs, but little had been accomplished thus far compared to the sheer scale of the destruction. It might take years before it was restored to its former condition.

"Ho! Reynard," a familiar voice called out.

Reynard searched the crowd of knights who began taking Stephen away until he smiled in recognition at seeing two faces he did not think would appear here. "Wymar! Theobald!" Reynard jumped from his horse and ran the distance to his brothers. He was taken by each man into a fierce embrace before the three men stood in a circle holding onto each other's forearms.

"He's grown another foot, I swear," Theobald teased before reaching out to rumple Reynard's hair as he had done since they were but children.

Wymar did the same. "Obviously all my worries that he was

not getting enough to fill his belly was for naught."

Reynard grinned before he smoothed down his hair. "At least I will not grow fat whiling away my time in a castle with naught to do," he said laughing and then watched while his oldest brother scowled at him whilst patting his lean stomach.

Theobald gave his little brother a small shove. "Just as cheeky as ever. Have you been behaving yourself?"

Reynard stood firm upon his feet. "Of course. I am on business of much import for our empress."

Wymar had one brow rise, causing Reynard to inwardly prepare himself for whatever words would follow. "We had a brief conversation with Richard when he arrived just ahead of you. He tells us differently."

Reynard narrowed his eyes. "Mayhap Richard has told you a falsehood."

Wymar chuckled. "I highly doubt it, but we have plenty of time to catch up. See to your horse and meet us in the tavern for food and a drink."

"Which tavern?" Reynard asked looking around trying to find a building that still stood intact.

Theobald ran his hand through his hair. "The only one that is left. Not easy to miss. We shall see you shortly… that is if you can tear yourself away from a certain lady."

Reynard growled a curse causing both brothers to laugh at Reynard's expense. While it was certainly good to see his brothers, their arrival had been a complete surprise. He could only ponder what was in store for him during his brief stay in Winchester.

※

CHAPTER TWELVE

Elysande held the edges the hood of her cloak together against the wind threatening to blow the covering off her head. The night was cold and brisk, and she could see her breath as she hurried across what was left of Winchester toward the tavern. Her hand held tight to the crook of Hawke's arm whilst Olive followed close behind. She was in unfamiliar territory with what she considered a grim future. Everything she had known and loved was left behind at Blackmore except for the two who had stayed by her side. Hawke was considered an ally. Olive had been no more than a servant in her household and yet now both had become so much more. They were a lifeline to her past and their friendship would need to carry her into her unknown future.

There was no need for sparkling conversation as they hastened their steps to find the warmth of the tavern. Elysande kept her head low and relied on Hawke's sense of direction to ensure that they were headed the right way. But when they at last espied the well-lit tavern, her feet stumbled when she heard male laughter. She had no idea what to expect once they entered since the only tavern she had ever been in was one located in the village of Blackmore. Even then, 'twas a rare occurrence for her to ever go inside.

Hawke held the door open for her and the rush of warm air coming from the hearth was a welcome relief after the coolness of the night. The tavern was crowded. She supposed this should not have come as any surprise considering Hawke had informed her that this was the only place to dine that had survived the fires that had razed the city.

Many of those she espied before her were familiar, having ridden her horse with them for the past two days. But there were also men who she had not seen before, and she assumed they lived here in the city or were traveling through as well on their own journeys. Some cast her a glance that made her uncomfortable and she stepped closer to Hawke for his protection.

They finally saw Reynard across the room, who waved them forward. As they neared, he motioned to the vacant places at his table.

"Come and join us, Lady Elysande, and let me introduce you to my brothers," Reynard said in a cheerful voice.

Brothers? she thought whilst placing a small smile upon her face as their names blurred whilst she attempted to gain control of her uneasiness. She had no idea that she would be introduced to his brothers or even that they would also be here in Winchester. But then again, she had not been on speaking terms with Reynard since their kiss at Bristol. How could she have known his brothers would be here, too?

When a chalice of wine had been set before her, she raised her eyes whilst taking a sip to watch the three men across from her. Their similarities were close enough that she could see the resemblance in their features to prove they were related. At first glance, Wymar seemingly was the most different from the other two brothers, but in truth 'twas only due to the color of his hair. 'Twas a lighter shade of brown than the other two men whose tresses were darker. Theobald had a small scar running down his left cheek, causing Elysande to ponder if it had happened whilst in some battle. Reynard clearly was the youngest of the three.

Hawke took her hand underneath the table and gave it a small squeeze, and then answered for Elysande since she had missed the entire conversation whilst silently observing the brothers.

"Lady Elysande has been surviving remarkably well considering the circumstances," Hawke replied before he began eating from the food set between them on the trencher they were to share.

A grunt left Reynard. "Is that what you call it, Hawke? She could barely feed herself let alone the rest of you who stayed with her."

Elysande raised her eyes to peer at Reynard. "I am sitting right here… you can address me directly, sir."

Reynard shrugged before he took a mouthful of venison and began to chew. He finally answered her after he swallowed and wiped his mouth on the back of his sleeve. "Since we have fallen out of accord, I assumed you would prefer that I speak through Hawke."

Wymar leaned forward. "Watch your manners in front of the lady, Reynard."

"I have done nothing wrong," he said with a scowl of disapproval.

Elysande took another sip of her wine. "There is no need to come to my defense, Lord Wymar. I assure you that although your brother and I have had our differences in the brief time we have known one another I have become used to his… moods. I am certain we can tolerate one another and remain civil for at least one meal."

A laugh from Theobald erupted as he banged his fist on the table in merriment. "I believe you may have met your match, Reynard," he teased. "'Tis about time you encountered a woman who would not put up with your foul temper."

"Hear, hear," Wymar added raising his tankard of ale. "A toast to the Lady Elysande… a rare beauty among women, with a brave spirit to match."

Everyone raised their cup in a toast whilst Elysande could feel a blush of embarrassment rush across her face. She was unused to such treatment of late and was not certain she deserved such accolades to be raised on her behalf.

Hawke pushed the trencher closer to her. She began to eat

her fill while conversations swirled around her.

"What brings you to Winchester?" Hawke inquired in curiosity.

Theobald thumped Reynard's shoulder. "You mean besides keeping abreast of what this young scamp is up to?"

"Shut up, Theo," Reynard muttered, taking a quick glance at Elysande from beneath his lashes.

"Aye," Hawke returned, waiting for the reply.

Wymar rested his forearms on the edge of the table. "I would think it would be obvious, but we are here to ensure there is a calm exchange between the prisoners. One can only pray that this will happen on the morrow peacefully. There has been enough bloodshed between enemies of late."

"And then?" asked Olive when she set down her goblet.

Theobald gave her a wink. "And then, Wymar and I will return to Bristol to ensure Queen Matilda and those with her are also released in a peaceful manner. After that, the two of us will return home to the lovely wives who await us.

"Oh!" Olive said in what sounded like a disappointed tone. She appeared saddened to learn that both men had commitments elsewhere. She began to also eat her fill and no longer contributed to the men's conversations.

"Aye..." Reynard grumbled into his tankard of ale." Marital bliss. I wish my brothers both well with such an endeavor."

A smirk lifted at the corners of Wymar's lips. He turned his blue-grey eyes to Elysande and then his youngest sibling before he at last commented. "One day you shall know the love of a good woman, Reynard. Until then, 'tis best that you treat those who you escort with respect, especially if she may one day be one of the empress's attendants."

"I have treated Lady Elysande with respect," he said in a snarl.

Elysande hid her laughter behind her chalice of wine. 'Twas clear that these brothers were close but also that Reynard's temper was something the older two were well aware of. She could only ponder what the cause was, not that his temperament should overly worry her or be cause for concern. She only had to endure the man for as long as it took them to travel to Oxford, and then she would be well rid of his company. Still… she did wonder.

Setting her cup down, her gaze traveled to the oldest Norwood brother. "How did you meet your wife, Lord Wymar?" she asked.

Another jovial chuckle left Theobald. "An interesting story…"

"Aye," Wymar replied with a smile. He seemed lost in the memory of his wife for a moment before he returned his attention to Elysande. "I suppose originally I met her prior to the Battle of Lincoln, although at the time I only knew her as a young knight needing aid."

"The lady was hardly in need of your aid, Wymar, nor did she want it if I recall," Theobald said thumping his tankard on the table.

"She fought in a battle?" Elysande inquired with wide eyes. She could not even image herself in such a place let alone hefting a sword to defend herself.

Wymar pointed to his brother. "As did Theobald's lady, Ingrid."

"You met them both at Lincoln?" she asked.

Theobald shook his head. "Nay, I found my lady on her way here to Winchester to give aid to the empress's cause," he declared. "I took her under my wing to ensure she was well protected."

"I can hardly fathom a woman on a battlefield," she murmured.

Reynard was not to be left out of the conversation. "Aye. Both ladies are rare in both beauty and their skills with a sword."

Elysande turned her head to stare at Reynard. Those steel grey eyes seemingly bored into her own. "You met them both?"

"Aye. Long before my brothers were wed, we made a vow to stay together and fight side by side for our empress. But once they found love, the empress decided that they could best serve her by settling down with their wives. Now I travel with Lord Richard who is as much a brother to me as these two."

Richard leaned forward on the table. "I have apparently taken up the cause of ensuring the youngest Norwood brother continues to stay out of trouble and does not leave too much havoc in his wake."

Laughter erupted from the men who were seated around her. Not only were these men close because of their vow to the empress, but there was a camaraderie between them that linked them all as brothers of their hearts. 'Twas to be commended that they had remained close through the strife of their lives.

As the evening wore on, tales of battles and women loved and lost began to spill from the men's mouths. Elysande laughed along with them even though she knew these stories had been filtered to be suitable for a lady's hearing. She stifled a yawn and looked toward the tavern door to see if Hawke had returned from escorting Olive to her rooms for the night. But the door remained shut and she wondered how long it would take before she, too, could find her sleep for the night.

Wymar took matters into his own hands. "Reynard... the lady is in much need of finding her rest. Be a good lad and escort her back to her room at the castle," he demanded with a wave of his hand. With his edict delivered, he turned back to his conversation with Richard.

Reynard stood and made his way around the table before he held out his arm. "My lady... shall we?" he asked far more politely than she expected.

Elysande stood and gave a short curtsey. "Gentlemen... I bid you a good eve," she said before taking Reynard's arm.

She tried her best to remain calm but once again her heart betrayed her. She could only hope she could make her way across the short distance to where she would spend the night without making a complete fool of herself. She pondered how many times she would need to remind herself that she would not fall under this man's spell!

~~~~~~

CHAPTER THIRTEEN

REYNARD CLOSED THE door of the tavern whilst Elysande waited next to him. A gust of air came upon them causing the hood of her cloak to fall from her head. Before he could stop himself, he reached over to grab hold of the fabric and return it to its rightful place. Standing this close to the woman, he breathed in the scent of roses and was momentarily lost in the memory of when they sat on a bench in a garden. He fastened the clasp at her neck to keep the cloak from opening further, and their hands touched as she, too, went to hold the garment in place.

"My thanks, Reynard," she said quietly.

Looking down upon her, for she was quite small in stature, he could not help thinking that those blue eyes would surely be his downfall. "You are most welcome, Elysande," he replied before he took her hand and placed it back in the crook of his arm.

They began their evening stroll back toward the castle and he felt her shiver from the cool night air. He took his own cloak and pulled the edge of it around her shoulder, bringing her closer to the warmth of his body. There was no reason they should both be cold when he could easily remedy the situation.

She did not protest their close proximity but she did stiffen a little, perhaps recalling the last time they had been so close. It caused him to realize he owed her an apology for his previous behavior. He halted their progress whilst still holding her close.

"Elysande…" he began but was not sure how to proceed with reliving his past with a woman who was mostly a stranger.
~~~~~~

She fingered the edges of his leather jerkin. "Reynard…" His name coming from her lips had him wondering why this woman continued to pull at his heart strings. True… she reminded him of Johanna but Elysande was more than just a memory of a woman he used to love. Elysande was real and staring upon him with what appeared as affection. Johanna could never be more than just a ghost of a memory of what would never be.

"I must needs apologize for my earlier behavior," he began in a rush.

"Men will be men when they are into their cups I suppose," she said softly misunderstanding his words, apparently thinking he was apologizing for their conversation in the tavern.

"'Tis not what I meant, Elysande."

"Then what?"

He gave a heavy sigh, finding the strength to answer when a different pair of blue eyes flashed unbidden in his memory. "The garden…"

"I see…" Her words trailed off as if she, too, relived the memory of their kiss.

"You never gave me the opportunity to allow me to explain about—"

"You do not owe me any explanation. I was the one at fault and should not have pushed myself at you," she said interrupting his attempt at an apology.

He shook his head. "Nay… you were not at fault, Elysande. 'Twas the memory of my past that caused my stupidity to utter another's name."

She stepped back from the warmth of his body and he felt the loss when cold air rushed between them as his cloak fell from her shoulders.

"You love her," she said stating the obvious.

"Loved. She passed from this world many years ago," he said, and he saw what he assumed was concern wash over her face.

"Yet you love her still."

"I suppose I do in many ways. I made a vow the day she died

that I would never allow myself to love again."

A gasp left her lips before a frown formed upon her brow. "You made a vow upon her death years ago?" she asked crossing her arms over her chest as if to give herself support.

"Aye." What else could he say since she spoke the truth of the matter?

A sound escaped her. "You must have been extremely young then, for you cannot be much older than my score of years."

He shrugged. "I am three and twenty."

She shuffled her foot in the dirt underneath her. "'Tis hard to believe that you would hold yourself to such a vow made not only at such a young age but also whilst grief consumed you."

"Death affects us all differently. Surely you understand given that you are also grieving," he muttered. What did it matter that he had been young when he had loved and lost Johanna? He had been well old enough to understand the pain that love could bring. What measure of fool would he be to condemn himself to that pain again? Nay, love was not for him. Though he knew he would likely wed one day, he would wed sensibly, for the benefit of his family and his empress. Love would not enter the matter.

"I am grieving for a beloved grandfather, not someone I was in love *with,* and therein lies the difference," she murmured in what sounded like disbelief before she continued. "But this does not lessen the death of someone you cared for. I am sorry for your loss, Reynard, and hope that you will one day learn to let love into your heart again."

"You accept my apology?" he inquired, holding out his arm again for them to continue their walk.

Blue eyes turned up to gaze upon him again, and he swore he saw a hint of disappointment in her features before a mask slid down into place. "Aye. I can also assure you that you have no need to fear that I will make another attempt at kissing you, especially knowing you still grieve for your loved one. Besides… my attempt was a complete failure."

A chuckle left him, causing her chin to lift in anger at what she must have seen as mockery. He hastened to explain. "I was not making fun of you, Elysande, only that your kiss was far from a failure. In fact, you made me forget myself... and the vow I had whilst I held you in my arms."

"I did?" she asked with wide eyes.

"Aye, you did, and if I am not careful, I might forget myself and kiss you again," he said with what he hoped sounded like a sincere heart.

She halted their progress when they reached the keep door and she placed her hand over his heart. "Until you are free from the memory of your beloved, there will be no kissing or anything else between us. I will not be a replacement for someone nor be mistaken again for another woman. I deserve more than to be regarded as second to a ghost."

"I understand," he said with a slight bow of his head knowing there would not be any further moonlit kisses coming from the lady before him. Unless he wanted a serious relationship with Elysande, he would need to allow her to move on with her life wherever it may take her.

Her smile was weak at best, but she took his arm once more when he opened the portal before them. "In the meantime, let us be friends. There are not many whom I am close to, and one can never have enough friends in their lives, do you not agree?" she declared whilst it appeared as though she forced a smile on her lips.

"Aye... friends," he choked out wondering how on earth he would remain friends with a woman. Those he came across in his past were only used for the purpose to ease his needs and not for any sort of permanent relationship. They were tavern wenches or those to be found in camp when their tents were set up near a battlefield. Aside from them, the women he had spent the most time with were the brides of his brothers. And whilst they were beautiful, remarkable women, their feelings for Wymar and Theobald had been so readily apparent from early on that he had never truly thought of them as women. To him, nearly from the start, they had been sisters. But Elysande was no sister—not at all.

Making their way inside, he followed her up the turret stairs, down a long drafty passageway, and then halted before her bedchamber door. She patted his arm and put her hand on the handle before pushing the solid wood open.

"Good eve to you, Sir Reynard," she said quietly returning to a more formal way to address him. He was not sure that he cared for the formality.

"May you sleep well, Lady Elysande," he replied with a bow.

The door closed and he rested his hand on the wood separating him from the woman who continued to surprise him. His mind flitted through their conversation until he finally turned and walked away.

Friends? With a woman? God's Bones. He was doomed!

CHAPTER FOURTEEN

T HE SOUND OF laughter above the minstrels who played in the empress's great hall filled the room. Knights and their ladies danced to a merry tune and wine and food filled the banquet tables as everyone celebrated Christmas day. 'Twas hard to believe that Elysande had resided here at Oxford for almost a month. It seemed like yesterday that she had arrived in the bailey of this castle.

She and Hawke had remained in Winchester after the prisoner exchange went peacefully. She had been thankful that no further bloodshed had occurred between all the parties involved. She also could not have been happier that she would no longer have to lay eyes on King Stephen… the murdering cur! After all, he was the reason why she was here in the first place after his army left her home in shambles.

She had thought she would continue traveling in Reynard's company, but he had other ideas. He had explained there was no sense in her traipsing back to Bristol to oversee the release of Queen Matilda only to return here to ensure Earl Robert's heir gained his freedom. Elysande could only wait for his return before they at last began making their way to Oxford.

Word had traveled quickly that Stephen would once again be crowned as King of England. If the empress felt any pangs of displeasure at the news, she kept them well hidden from those who resided with her here at Oxford. Elysande was treated as any other guest who remained loyal to the empress and had not as yet been ordered to attend her. On many accounts she was thankful to be allowed the freedom to see to her own daily schedule as she desired instead of having to spend every waking hour attending the empress. Whilst this may be considered an honor, Elysande was not entirely sure she would be able to stand such a position.

Her eyes went to Richard's sister Beatrix who stood behind the empress's chair. The poor woman appeared completely bored and as if to prove Elysande's thoughts, the girl quickly hid a yawn. Elysande stifled a giggle. Beatrix had been a delightful surprise upon Elysande's arrival at Oxford. Richard had immediately introduced them. The same age as Reynard, Beatrix was a trifle bit... determined... Elysande supposed was the best way to describe her, and mayhap a little spoiled after getting her way far too often. But while she could be stubborn and impetuous, she was also spirited and engaging, and Elysande appreciated the friendship that was beginning to develop between them.

"You appear far too deep into your thoughts, my lady," Reynard said when he leaned down to whisper in her ear.

Surprised that the man had sneaked up on her, she turned on the bench far too quickly and came face to face with the man who continued to fill her dreams. Those steel grey eyes sparkled mischievously at her causing Elysande's heart to once again betray her. No matter how many times she told herself to move on from her feelings toward Reynard, she could not help the attraction that continued to consume her.

"Nothing to concern yourself with, Sir Reynard. Just worried that Lady Beatrix might doze off whilst attending our empress," she said with a light laugh even though her heart was beating so rapidly the entire crowd would surely hear it for themselves.

The deep baritone of his laughter increased her smile knowing she was the cause. "Poor Beatrix," he chuckled before he took a seat next to her. "I am certain she is not pleased she is only one among many ladies who flirt with the men here at court or take part in the dancing. She is used to being the center of attention."

"The celebration for Christmas is magnificent. I have not seen this much revelry in many a year," Elysande exclaimed as she turned her attention to those who danced.

"Not even at Blackmore?" he asked with one raised dark brow.

Elysande shook her head but kept her attention on the dancing. She didn't trust herself to look into his face again. "Nay. My parents have been in Normandy for over a year now and left Blackmore for me to handle. But even prior to their current trip, they were rarely at home. They have spent many years… absent from my life, to put it as politely as possible. I love them but they are very single minded in enjoying their own lives together without the burden of a child and the responsibilities that come with it."

He took her hand and raised it to his lips. "A pity… they are missing out on your lovely company." He continued holding her hand until she had little choice other than to finally gaze upon him.

It was her downfall. Her breath hitched. Her hand tingled where he continued to rub his thumb over her skin. Her mouth became dry and all she could think about was leaning forward and kissing his lips.

She cleared her throat as though this would help her to remain indifferent to the spell he was unknowingly weaving around them. She was the one who told him they would be friends. She needed to keep to the plan to remain civil and not ruin what she herself put into place.

"A son…" she muttered not finishing her thoughts on the matter.

"A son?" he asked with a frown.

"Aye… they were disappointed I was female and thus would not carry on my father's name. My mother was unable to have any other children after she almost died giving birth to me." Her explanation rushed from her mouth and for a moment all the loneliness of her childhood came rushing to the forefront of her mind.

As the daughter of the lord and lady of Blackmore, she was kept apart from the village girls and had learned from an early age the responsibilities that came with her position in life. It stood to reason this was why she had thought she had fallen in love with her captain of her guard. He was with her as a constant reminder that she was different and of noble birth. Her blue eyes left Reynard's and traveled to see Hawke across the hall. She had an older brother in her captain and was thankful for his continued presence. If only her grandfather yet lived…

"'Tis their loss, Elysande, and mayhap they will come around and appreciate all you have done to try to keep Blackmore running," he said with such positivity that she wished his words might come true. But she knew her parents and she highly doubted they would change their ways anytime soon.

She formed her mouth into a grim line of displeasure. "I wish I had your confidence, Reynard, but such a miracle might only occur with the second coming. They are very set in their ways."

He took her hand once more and gently pulled her to her feet. "Come! This is no time to be so melancholy and I refuse to be the cause. Let us dance, my lady, and make merry!"

She had no time to argue his decision because before she could reply he was whirling her around the hall to the pattern of the dance. She forgot anything else she had been pondering outside of enjoying the moment of being in his arms. She knew it would not last for long and she would take this time unto herself to just be happy no matter how briefly such an emotion would last.

When he lifted her around her waist and brought her high, she swore it seemed as though her joy lifted to the heavens. With her hands resting upon his shoulders, she tilted her head back smiling as he spun her in a circle. But that smile quickly faded when he slowly brought her back down and her body slid along his muscular form. Their eyes met upon her descent until her feet touched the floor. Her knees buckled and he quickly tightened his hold upon her, bringing her into his embrace. They stood there in silence staring at one another both with wide eyes. The contact of their bodies had been like an awakening and Elysande could only stand there in wonder knowing Reynard felt it, too.

"May I dance with the lady?" a male voice said breaking the spell between them.

Elysande quickly stepped back from Reynard for propriety's sake, hiding the fact that she was disappointed by the interruption and the fact that another wished to dance with her.

Reynard bowed low. "Of course," he replied before taking her hand and raising her quaking limb to his lips. "Thank you for the dance, Lady Elysande."

She gave a nod of her head. "Sir Reynard…"

Elysande watched him go until the stranger before her took her about the waist and they continued with the dance. This man's hair was as black as the midnight sky and he had eyes so green they reminded her of the deepest part of the forest at Blackmore. He was slightly shorter than Reynard but just as muscular. Another warrior whose fealty was sworn to the empress, she supposed.

"We have not been introduced," Elysande finally murmured when the silence stretched between them.

One dark brow rose as though to say she should know his name and was put out that she was not familiar with him. But to her, he was just one among many who stayed here at Oxford Castle. She had not met every man and woman here, especially for the holiday.

"Constantine Warin, Earl of Charlbury," he replied with a nod of his head as he continued to lead her through the patterns of the dance. They broke apart and then returned to clasp hands.

"My lord," she said as they turned in a circle. "I am Lady Elysande Thorburn of Blackmore."

"I know who you are." His reply was curt but mayhap that was because they were forced to once again break apart.

When they came together again, she was once more lifted high but this time her reaction was far different than when

Reynard had performed this same move. Her gaze traveled to the man who continued to twirl her around, but all Elysande could think of was she wished Reynard was still the man dancing with her. Her feet touched the floor and she instantly wished for the music to come to an end.

When the last notes were played by the minstrels, Elysande found her hand tucked into the crook of Lord Constantine's arm as he began to escort her from the floor. She thought he would return her to where she had been seated but instead he took her to stand near a wall where they were, for the most part, alone.

"I have had my eyes on you since your arrival here at Oxford, my lady," Constantine finally drawled.

That this stranger had been watching her caused the hair on the back of her neck to rise. "I am hardly anyone noteworthy, my lord," she said keeping her tone civil even whilst her gaze traveled the room in search of Hawke or even Reynard.

"I was surprised our empress did not take you under her wing and have you attend her. 'Tis an honor to become one of her ladies in waiting," he said with a wave of his hand.

"I am certain the empress has her reasons, and naturally I would not dream of questioning her as to what that may be," Elysande answered but frowned when he stepped closer.

"You should make yourself more available to her," he suggested and took her hand. "'Twill do you no harm to put yourself before her whenever the opportunity arises."

"I am certain the empress will call me to her if she has need of me. I do not see how following her every move and interfering will do me any good… not that I need help of any kind."

Constantine waved his free hand. "Everyone is eager to gain Empress Matilda's favor. 'Tis the way of court life that you should adhere to. How else are you to become one of her attendants?"

"I am perfectly capable of making my own decisions on where my life will lead, my lord," she scoffed, attempting to pull her hand away. This man was making her uncomfortable, and she wished to leave his side without causing a scene.

A disbelieving chuckle left him. "You would be wise to heed my words. I heard your precious Blackmore is all but falling down and in need of many repairs. You will need monies lining your coffers to ensure you can restore your estate to what it once was. For that, you will need a husband who is wealthy for such a miracle to happen *and* the empress's help."

"I do not need a husband to restore my land to its former glory," she said miffed that this was what most men thought. What made them so obstinate in the belief that a woman could never make it on her own without the assistance of a husband?

He pulled her closer. "Aye. You do. And if you stop to think hard about the prospect of marrying you would see 'twill be the solution to most of your problems. I think we would suit."

She yanked her hand from his hold and stepped back. "You do not even know me."

Constantine shrugged. "There will be plenty of time to get to know each other after we are wed. In fact, I have already proposed the idea to the empress."

She gasped at the prospect of being wed to such an egotistical man who seemed to feel he had the right to take over her life. "You presume too much, sir," she fumed.

A smirk turned up at the corner of his lips. "I know you must be overwhelmed at the thought of marrying me. But my own estate is not far from Oxford, and I am wealthy enough in my own right. An added bonus to our union is that I have the empress's ear. We would do well together."

She could only stand there in disbelief. Her eyes traveled to the empress sitting on her throne, and Elysande gulped when the empress raised her chalice toward the pair of them in a silent toast. She could not marry the earl. She could live a hundred years and in her heart she would never be able to love him.

CHAPTER FIFTEEN

Reynard watched Elysande from the distance separating them and scowled. He did not like how close Warin was standing next to the lady nor did he care for the fact that their own dance had been interrupted by one who was close to the empress. He wanted to interrupt the pair but did he have the right to do so? Nay. He knew he did not, much to his annoyance.

Blake nudged him out of his stupor. "Are you just going to stand by and not go to the lady's rescue?"

"Aye… not very chivalrous of you," Kingsley agreed with a laugh.

Oswin stepped closer to the group. "She does not appear pleased with whatever their conversation is about."

A growl rumbled in Reynard's chest. "Leave me be," he grumbled, taking a sip of his wine even as his eyes remained on Elysande.

Richard held out his goblet and it was refilled by a passing servant. "'Tis best to leave all matters where Lady Elysande is concerned to Warin. I hear there is an understanding between them. I believe the empress approves of a union between the pair.

"What?" Reynard erupted. The men around him began talking at the same time.

Richard held up his hand. "'Tis only a rumor at the moment, but you know how quickly these things happen and can escalate here at court. Besides," he turned his blue eyes directly to stare at Reynard, "a match with Warin will ensure she can restore

Blackmore. If not Warin, there are others who I have heard are interested in making a match with the lady."

Blake frowned. "Warin is an arse and full of himself. The lady could do much better."

Oswin laughed. "With who? You?"

The men chuckled when Blake cursed. "I did not say I was interested in the lady *that* way."

All eyes turned in Reynard's direction. "There is nothing between Elysande and I. We are merely friends."

Richard stepped forward to place one hand upon Reynard's shoulder. "I would say you lie, my friend. The looks exchanged between you and the lady whilst you danced told anyone who looked close enough that you care for each other."

Reynard gulped hard. "I cannot give her what she needs."

Richard nodded to the other men present. "Leave us," he ordered. Once they complied he turned once more to Reynard.

"I suppose you feel the need to impart some words of wisdom, Richard, so get it over with," Reynard grumbled. He raked his hand through his hair and then took another gulp of wine.

"If you care at all for Lady Elysande, I highly suggest you speak to our empress and express your interest in the lady as soon as possible. Otherwise, you may lose more than... as you say... a friend. 'Tis time you let go of the past and allow yourself to live life to its fullest potential. Lady Elysande could be the woman of your dreams, Reynard. Keep the memory of Johanna in your heart but I think 'tis far past time that you allow yourself to fall in love again."

Richard got straight to the point he wanted to make, and Reynard shot him a look of indifference, causing the brother of his heart to chuckle. "What do you know of finding a woman who you could love?" Reynard shot back. "I do not see you falling into the trap of such an emotion that only causes havoc in our lives."

"Mayhap I have not come across a woman who would be my match..." Richard got a far-off look that Reynard had seen on his brothers' faces before. He straightened up, realizing that this pointed to the idea that perhaps Richard *had* actually come across such a paragon of virtue: a woman worthy of him.

"Ha!" he exclaimed, pointing toward Richard. "You have seen a woman that held your interest. Who is she?"

Richard shook his head apparently clearing his musings. "I have no idea. I caught but a brief glimpse of a woman during the siege of Winchester. In fact, Theobald's lady wife allowed the woman to go free. I took chase once I felled the enemy before me but she disappeared."

"And now you, too, dream of a woman you cannot have," Reynard teased with a smirk of satisfaction.

"Well… I can hardly lay some claim upon a woman I only briefly observed during the heat of battle but I *was* intrigued by her. There are not many women who would place themselves in the middle of a war," Richard replied with a shrug.

"Why do you not go and find her?" Reynard asked.

"You know as well as I do that I am not free to do so. Not while I am still in service to our empress. Besides, where would I even begin to look? The siege was months ago, and she could be anywhere."

"In the meantime, we remain miserable thinking of women who weave a spell around us and only leave us wanting for what cannot be," Reynard answered, then took another sip of wine. "I hate the feeling of being trapped."

"I suppose I may one day chance upon her and there may be hope. Wymar and Theobald do not seem to mind that they have found their women. It cannot be all bad. For that reason, I would hardly call love a trap. Besides, your lady is only a few steps away. You only need to cross the space and let your intentions be known. If you do not, someone else will lay claim to her."

Reynard set his cup down whilst his eyes roamed the distance between himself and Elysande. When he saw Elysande yank her hand from Warin's, the last shreds of his self-control snapped within him. "Excuse me, Richard," he muttered.

"Wise choice," Richard exclaimed and Reynard swore he heard Richard's laughter when he left his side.

When he finally crossed the room to stand before Warin and Elysande, did he detect a look of gratitude shining in the lady's eyes? He held out his hand and without hesitation Elysande slid her fingertips into his palm.

"I believe this next dance belongs to me. You will excuse us, of course, Lord Constantine," Reynard said and he pulled Elysande to stand beside him. He never gave Warin the chance for a reply even though the scowl the man gave him spoke volumes. Warin was not pleased but Reynard could not care less.

He did not take Elysande to start the next dance however. Instead, he continued through the great hall, past the main entrance of the keep, and continued through the castle until he came upon what served as a library. He bolted the door ensuring their privacy.

"What are you doing, Reynard? We should not be here alone. What will people think?" she whispered. But despite her protests, she made no move to unbolt the door. Instead, she backed up further into the room.

"I do not care what people think," he mumbled still irritated at how close Warin had been standing near Elysande.

She turned away from him. "The empress will not be pleased if what Lord Constantine just informed me is true."

He rushed to her side and turned her to face him. Witnessing the tears cascading down her cheeks caused something to lurch in his chest. He rubbed his thumbs over the wetness as he brushed it away. "What did that cad say to you to cause your tears?" he asked quietly before he took hold of both her hands.

"He said he has spoken to the empress about a possible match between us," she choked out. "I cannot marry a man I do not know or love." Her tears began anew whilst she hid her face in her hands. God's Blood… 'Twas worse than he thought and now he knew for certain Richard had spoken the truth but a short while ago.

"Most marriages are arranged thusly," he uttered but the moment his words left his mouth, he knew with a certainly he should not have said them.

"But 'tis not how I imagined mine!" she sobbed. "Since my parents were never around, my grandfather swore I would be able to choose whomever I wished to marry. He prayed it would be for love and not for my monies that would one day line a man's coffers, not that there was anything left of those funds after Stephen's men ransacked Blackmore." Her tears continued whilst she tried to take in gulps of air.

"Your grandsire was a wise man." He pulled her into his arms, running his fingers down the length of her silky hair. "We shall think of something," he murmured trying to ease her pain and feeling a part of him shatter knowing she was hurting.

She pulled from his arms. "I have no idea what can be done. I am about to be but a pawn in a game played by others where some *man* gains the title to my lands," she sneered before she went over to a desk and began fidgeting with several objects. The quill, the inkwell, several pieces of parchment were hastily picked up, then put back down as if to distract her from the reality of her life. But 'twas the stick of red wax that snapped in two that caused her to throw the remains back on top of the desk in frustration. Her hands clasped the edge of the desk whilst her head hung in what he knew was despair.

"I can talk to the empress—"

"And tell her what?" she bellowed, turning to face him. Her hands became fists at her sides before she continued. "Will you ask to take his place? Commit yourself to me as you did to Johanna?"

"I do not know that she would give us permission to wed since I do not have the wealth and security that Warin could offer you," he said honestly and for the first time in his entire life, he wished that things could be different. Wymar had had the family's name and lands rightfully returned to him, which was as it should be. Theobald had been forced to wed but it turned out to be a love match and he gained more than just a wife with his union to Ingrid. But where did this leave Reynard without his own title and lands? He supposed he was at the mercy of the empress and what she might bestow upon him, but he did not wish Elysande to think he would only wed her for what she, too, would bring him.

Another sob escaped Elysande before she squared her shoulders and wiped away her tears. She came to him and placed her hand upon his cheek. "If only things were different and we had perchance met in some other place in time. You would be so easy to love if you were to open your heart to me, Reynard…"

Her words trailed away and she offered him the smallest of smiles. Going onto the tips of her toes, her hands went to his shoulders, and she leaned forward and placed a chaste kiss upon his cheek before she fled from his side.

The sound of the bolt sliding to allow her to leave caused him to turn, but he only had time enough to watch her rush through the door once she opened it. He should have gone after her but somehow he could not move. The warmth of her lips upon his cheek had almost been his undoing and suddenly the vow he made to himself years ago no longer mattered. Nothing mattered but somehow having Elysande in his life. Somehow Elysande had crept into his heart and he wanted her to stay there. He would speak with the empress at the first opportunity. He could not have his lady marry another…

✦ ❦ ✦

CHAPTER SIXTEEN

E LYSANDE TRIED TO keep her gaze forward when she was brought before the Empress in her solar. The room was filled with knights and her lady attendants. Reynard and Richard stood against a wall near a window and were as still as any marble statue that Elysande had ever seen. There was a brief moment when Reynard's steel grey eyes flickered to meet hers when she entered but now there was not any sign of emotion from him... absolutely nothing.

Reynard and Richard were not the only ones she recognized. Blake Kennarde and Kingsley Goodee were also present, as was Constantine Warin who hovered relatively close to the Empress. A sly grin and a slight nod of his head told Elysande much. Whatever the reason she had been summoned to the empress and this chamber, Constantine had been informed and was pleased about it. Her eyes took in the rest of the knights who were here as they all began to bow. Some she had danced with during her time here at Oxford Castle. Others, she had been introduced to even if she barely knew anything about them. The world of the court was still strange to her—so different from the quiet life she had left behind.

"You must be wondering why I have brought you to my solar, Lady Elysande," the empress began, sitting down in a chair that dominated the room. Another throne for the lady's pleasure and to show she was in charge of all.

"I am at your service, my Empress," Elysande murmured

bowing her head. When she raised her eyes, they met Beatrix's and there was no way Elysande could miss the concern that washed over the lady's visage. Something was happening that involved her, and she could only dread what was about to happen to change her life once more.

The empress drummed her fingers on the arm of her chair until her gaze swept the room. "As Lord Constantine informed you—without gaining my permission first…" her head turned whilst one brow rose in his direction to show her displeasure, "he has asked to take you as his wife."

"Please, my Empress…" Elysande began but the lady held up her hand to halt any further protests.

"He is not the only one who has come before me to attempt to lay some claim upon you," the empress said with a slight smirk. "Norwood has also done so. He is one of my most faithful knights, but he and Constantine are not your only potential suitors. Several of my other nobles who are in this room have also expressed interest."

Elysande turned her attention to Reynard but he continued to stand at attention, still without any sort of emotion lighting his face. That he had gone before their empress to ask to marry her filled her soul with joy but there was still more here and she was afraid what might come next. The empress continued.

"Grancourt would make a suitable husband for you, but he has assured me his affections lie in another direction—not that I believe such a falsehood. But that is of little matter when there are other men who have stepped forward to be considered. So now all that rests is to make my choice as to what response I should give." The empress stood and began to pace. "I have thought long and hard on what I might do to resolve such a situation with so many vying for your hand, Lady Elysande."

"I continue to be your most humble servant," Elysande said quietly. What else could she say? Whatever was about to happen, she could do nothing but obey.

"You are more than aware of how those who have sworn

their fealty to me have suffered when the usurper and his men ransacked the land in their wake. Castles lie in ruins along with their fields, people are starving, and the winter months will be long and cold. You have experienced this yourself, have you not?"

"Aye. Blackmore is in desperate need of repair, Empress," Elysande said as she again surveyed the room of knights.

"Aye. Norwood has informed me of the condition of Blackmore and the reason he insisted you travel with him," the empress replied and she once again took a seat.

"I was most grateful for his… offer," Elysande replied and for the first time since her entrance, she saw the briefest hint of a grin light Reynard's face before the mask fell back into place.

"Since there are many who would make you a suitable husband, I have decided to have a tournament with the winner to be granted your hand in marriage." The empress seemed satisfied with her solution and sat back in her chair. "I am sure my people will enjoy a small diversion to distract them from the burden that fills their lives."

Elysande's mouth hung open in surprise before she snapped her lips shut. It was only then that she could find her voice and thoughts. "And when will this tourney occur?" she dared to ask, trying not to let her voice be colored by her disbelief that her life would be determined by the winner of a game.

"I will plan the occasion for the beginning of April. That should see most of the winter's snow gone from the land and will give you the next several months to spend time with your… suitors."

"April…" was the only word she could squeak out past her lips.

"I know… you are too overwhelmed to convey your gratitude for such a brilliant idea." The empress waved her hand in the air as if this tournament would be the answer to all of Elysande's problems. 'Twas so far from the truth of the matter that she wanted to run from the room.

"My Empress, if 'twould please you, I would like to ask you

to reconsider," Elysande said bravely, trying to hold on to her strength of will even though she knew such a suggestion would not go over well.

The empress sat forward again and gripped the arms of her chair. "Reconsider? Whatever for, dear girl? The people will have a tourney to attend to fill several days with merriment, and you shall find yourself a suitable husband who will be worthy of you. Why should I change my mind when I put a fair amount of thought into your future?" she warned with a frown.

"I only thought that mayhap—"

"You would do well to adhere to my suggestions, Lady Elysande, and become obedient to my directives," the empress commanded.

"Aye… of course, my Empress," Elysande said even as she swore her knees were about to buckle.

"Norwood," the empress said summoning her knight to come stand before her.

Reynard bowed. "My Empress," he declared, holding his position until he was ordered to rise.

"See that Lady Elysande is escorted to her chambers. I fear the surprise has been too much for her and that she must needs compose herself before the evening meal."

"'Twould be my pleasure," he answered holding out to Elysande. "My lady… shall we?"

Elysande took hold of the support Reynard offered after she curtsied to their monarch. The moment the door closed behind them, her knees gave way and she found herself once again in Reynard's arms.

"What am I to do?" she asked as despair washed over her like the darkest cloud.

"Obey, as we all must," Reynard suggested as he began to help her down the dimly lit passageway. Once they arrived at her bedchamber, he opened the door. She expected him to leave but instead he, too, entered the room and slid the bolt.

Elysande went over to a table that held a pitcher of wine and poured herself a chalice. Once she took a drink to calm her nerves, she offered the cup to Reynard. He stepped forward, taking hold of the goblet and then turned the cup so he could place his lips where hers had just touched the rim. A lover's gesture that was clearly deliberate and one she could not overlook.

"You asked to wed me," she said as the thought of becoming his wife filled her heart.

"Aye." He did not give any further explanation and she waited for him to continue. Instead, he gave a heavy sigh and returned the chalice to her without another word.

"You said you would speak to the empress, and you kept your word to me, Reynard. I appreciate that you made an attempt to ask for my hand," Elysande said, placing the cup back down on the table. The bedchamber seemingly grew small with this warrior towering over her in the room.

"As you saw for yourself, there were others who had already spoken to our empress," he finally declared. His words were not necessarily what she wished to hear and yet she appreciated that he spoke the truth all the same.

"I honestly do not understand why I am of such interest to those men. My holdings are small in comparison to others and are in need of extensive repairs. I can hardly be considered an eligible match when there are others who are far wealthier than I," she murmured whilst a frown formed on her brow. "Why me?"

Reynard stepped forward taking hold of a lock of her black hair. He twirled the tresses around in his fingers and Elysande held her breath pondering what he would do next. They were alone in her bedchamber and she knew she never should have allowed him to bolt the door, but she was not about to ask him to leave. His hand dropped off of her hair and he then took hold of her about her waist bringing them close. She swore she could feel the heat of his body and hers trembled knowing he was near.

"You are a rare beauty, Elysande Thorburn of Blackmore. Any man in his right mind would be happy to take you as his bride," he said whilst one of his long warm fingers traced its way down her cheek causing her to shiver in delight. Those steel grey eyes pulled her into his web, and she swore she was lost all over again.

"Including you, Reynard Norwood?" she dared to ask.

"Most assuredly, my lady," he said with a slight chuckle.

Her hands came to rest on his chest and she could feel his muscular build beneath the fabric of his tunic. "And what of Johanna?" she inquired softly knowing how much the woman of his past had meant to him.

"What about her?" He brought them closer, the feeling of his nearness so overwhelming that Elysande was barely able to hold on to her thoughts about another woman. But no, this was important. She needed an answer.

"You must know I have to ask. Will I only be a replacement for her?"

"Nay. You are the only woman in my life and Johanna is where she belongs. A distant memory and nothing more."

The right words, but did he mean them? Only time would prove the worth of them. For now, she could only move forward and live each day as it came. After all, Reynard would not be the only knight who wanted to wed her. But when his hands came up to cup her cheeks and he began bending forward, Elysande could only think of the kiss that was just waiting for her. Their breaths mingled on a heartbeat and as they stared into one another's eyes, she saw the future that awaited her with this man.

A heavy-handed knock on her door broke them apart and they heard Richard's voice on the other side of the portal, demanding Reynard return to their empress. He quickly placed a hasty kiss upon her lips before he headed toward the door.

"Reynard," she called out as his hand was about to slide open the bolt.

"Aye?"

"About the tournament…"

"What about the tourney?"

"What do you plan to do about it?" she finally asked, voicing her concerns that she would be married to some other stranger.

"Do about it?"

"Aye. What do you have planned?"

He came rushing back to her and kissed her hard as though taking possession of her this very day instead of months from now. She could only stare up at him in wonder when he finally let her make an attempt to catch her breath. 'Twas impossible for he had stolen it from her. She watched him return to the door to leave as she waited for his answer.

"I plan to win!" A cocky grin lit his entire face. He gave her a hasty salute and left her standing there in awe.

Her handsome knight had a plan after all and the coming months would be sheer torture whilst she awaited the day she would learn exactly who would be her husband.

CHAPTER SEVENTEEN

REYNARD REINED IN his horse at the approach to Oxford Castle. The winter months had all but crawled by and what little time he had been allowed to spend with Elysande had been mostly in the presence of others or during a dance in the great hall. Their moments together were fleeting and unfortunately there were other knights who constantly vied for her attention, hoping that she might favor them.

There had been many changes to Oxford's grounds in preparation of the upcoming tournament with tents erected with the standards of nobles flying to depict their houses. His return to the castle after leaving to travel to Devizes with the Empress had been impatiently awaited, at least on his part. They had been gone for far longer than he wished to be away from the lady who had all but crept into his heart.

But the empress had insisted Reynard travel with her to meet with her half-brother Earl Robert and her other advisers. That he had been privy to such private conversations should have humbled him but the news that he heard only warned that a resumption of this war between the empress and Stephen still lingered on the horizon.

Empress Matilda had admitted she would need to find another way to gain the throne, having come to the realization that England was not ready for her to rule. Her oldest son Henry recently celebrated his ninth birthday. She had learned that her husband Geoffrey had begun campaigning on their son's behalf.

Geoffrey had already been busy in his attempts to conquer all of Normandy in her absence whilst Matilda fought to gain England's throne. If Geoffrey were to succeed and become duke, he would then remain in this important position until Henry gained his majority, at which point he would then resign in his son's favor.

But until such a time, the empress's position was precarious. She did not have the resources for a convincing war against Stephen nor was the church on her side any longer. Their only solution was to raise more troops. The empress hated the idea of asking her husband for help, but she was left with no choice. A missive would be sent to Geoffrey but his response could take months to be received back in Oxford.

Now they had returned almost to the day when the empress had told those left behind to ready the grounds for the tournament. Reynard had not had the opportunity in the recent weeks to spend any time on training, and he felt weak, which would do him no good in his quest to win the various matches and become victorious. Much was at stake, and he was in no way willing to lose the fair Elysande.

As he entered the inner bailey, a vision flew from the keep's door and down the stairs as she ran to greet him. Her black hair floated in the air, making her look like an angel come down from the heavens.

"Reynard," she called out with a bright smile, and he leapt down from his horse as she flung herself into his arms. He lifted her and buried his nose in her hair to breathe in the scent of roses that always reminded him of her.

"Elysande… you have grown more beautiful since I last saw you," he said in a husky tone that made him wish they were behind closed doors.

"I have missed you," she whispered whilst she held tightly around his neck.

"I can see that you have, and such news brings me much pleasure, my lady," he replied with a chuckle before he handed the reins of his steed to a lad who took the animal toward the stable.

The empress's wagon halted in the courtyard and her voice called out to the pair. "I can see for myself who she favors, Norwood, but release the lady before I take you to task for mishandling the woman."

He stepped back and raised Elysande's hand to his lips. He gave her a wink and was pleased to see her smile brighten. "Forgive me, Empress, but I have missed the lady," Reynard proclaimed as he went to the wagon to help the empress down. Once he set her on her feet, she waved her finger at him.

"Just remember you are not wed to her yet. If you want her, then you best win at my games," the empress said as a warning but then she made the mistake of allowing a short laugh to escape her lips, making it clear she was more amused than annoyed.

"I plan to do just that, my Empress," Reynard said with a nod of his head.

The empress waved her hand to dismiss him whilst pulling a linen handkerchief from her sleeve. She pressed the cloth to her nose. "Off with you then but you best clean up before I see you next, Norwood. You smell like your horse."

"Of course, Empress," Reynard replied with a bow and watched as Elysande fell into a curtsey before the empress left them.

Elysande took his arm. "I have much to tell you."

"Can it not wait until I do as the empress bids and wash the dirt away? I am certain she was correct when she mentioned I am not fit company after my travels."

Elysande shook her head. "I care not for any of that, Reynard, only that you are back. Come with me…"

She gave him little choice as she firmly took hold of his hand. He followed her along as she made her way down a path and into a secluded area of the garden where they would be out of sight. Before he could guess her intent, she pressed herself fully against him and he experienced the bliss of every inch of her body nestled close to his own. A groan escaped him. Something so simple yet there was nothing simple about the fact that her breasts were pressed against his chest. He peered down at those creamy orbs where her cleavage was appearing above the neckline of her gown. She was going to be his undoing.

And then he lost all thought when her arms made their way up and around his neck. "Kiss me, Reynard," she whispered so softly he almost missed her words.

How could he refuse? Bending forward he captured her lips with his own and began to explore what she so willingly offered. Did he feel the world tilt on its axis when their tongues began to dance together? Aye, he did. Surely, somehow, his whole world just shifted for he could not imagine letting this woman belong to anyone else but him.

How long this exquisite torture went on he could not say. Time seemed to stand still. When he at last put a halt to their play, her lips were red and swollen. He knew he had done something right if her look said anything about how much she wished to continue.

"Why did you stop?" she asked with wide eyes.

"Any more and I would unman myself," he confessed and he pulled her once more fully against him so she could tell for herself how much he wanted her.

"Oh!" She appeared so innocent there could be no mistake the lady was a virgin. It pleased him to know there had been no other before him.

"Aye… Besides, I cannot take things further until you are mine."

Elysande gave a little shrug. "I would not mind, Reynard, and mayhap if the deed was done there would be no need for a tournament."

"I will not take you like *that*, Elysande." He gave her another quick kiss and stepped back before he forgot himself again. "We will be wed. I swear it."

"Mayhap you should not make such a promise," she murmured but there was a catch to her voice whilst uncertainty crept into her voice.

She suddenly looked so forlorn that Reynard became concerned with what had been going on in his absence. "Something has happened…"

He watched her take several deep breaths to control herself. "The men who wish to marry me have grown… bolder in the empress's absence."

A growl of outrage left him. "Has someone…"

Her eyes became wide. "Oh heavens… no… nothing that far, but they are making their intentions very clear."

"Who?" he growled out, not trusting himself further.

"Lord Constantine for certain, although he is not as badly behaved as some of the others. A Lord Gerold Morcant has become a most unpleasant person to be around," she said whilst her lips formed into a grim line of displeasure.

"Morcant?" he asked and watched whilst Elysande gave a nod. "He has made the rounds of the empress's court attempting to win the hand of one wealthy heiress after another. There is a reason why the empress has denied him. Do your best to stay clear of him."

"They are only two men of many who have tried to put me in a position where a tournament would not be necessary. They mean to do anything to have me as their wife. Be careful on the morrow when the tourney begins. I would not be surprised if they plan to cheat their way to become the victor."

"And what of Warin? Has he at least remained respectful or must I needs call the man out?" Reynard inquired whilst swiping his hand across the back of his neck in agitation that any man would take advantage of the fair lady.

"Whilst Lord Constantine continues to make his intentions known, his behavior has remained proper. Still, I have never come across such a pompous arse in my entire life," she muttered as she rolled her blue eyes.

A short chuckle left him. "Sounds as though Warin is the least of my worries," Reynard said confidently.

She came to him and placed her hand over his heart. "Promise me you shall be careful," she replied, waiting for his answer.

"I promise," he declared, sealing his vow with another sweet kiss.

Elysande seemed to be relieved, and he began to escort her back toward the keep, promising to see her at the evening meal. He wondered if the empress would allow him to be seated next to his lady whilst they dined this eve. He would find out soon enough.

CHAPTER EIGHTEEN

ELYSANDE RUSHED DOWN the turret stairs. She was late, but she had wanted to finish the embroidered ribbon she had been working on. A favor to bestow upon the knight whom she wished to win her hand. If only the empress had not deemed a tourney necessary. Why could she not allow her to choose her groom? Then she might already be wed to Reynard. Elysande supposed the empress had her reasons but how would she ever be able to marry anyone except the man who had captured her attention? She would be beyond miserable with anyone else but Reynard Norwood as her husband.

She picked up her pace after grabbing a bit of cheese from one of the tables in the great hall to break her fast. She had no time to sit down and eat something more substantial although her stomach rumbled in protest. Whether that was from hunger or what was to happen in the coming days remained to be seen.

The sun shone brightly in the morning sky, giving evidence that the time had come for her to be on the platform erected for the empress and those closest to their lady, Elysande amongst the many vying for even a hint of attention from Matilda. Picking up the hem of her blue gown, she ran through the inner bailey, out the barbican gate, and through the throng of people who came to witness the spectacle put on for their entertainment. Those who had suffered the most from the war that raged across England only cared that for a brief moment in time they could forget their woes and live in the moment of revelry.

Her eyes scanned the knights who would attempt to win her hand. Many gave a courtly bow when she passed them by but there was only one knight who held her interest. Her steps halted abruptly when she finally espied him. By St. Michael's wings! He was magnificent.

Stripped down to barely any clothing, Reynard's skin glistened in oil telling Elysande he would be in a wrestling match before aught else took place in the games. His stomach muscles were rippled whilst the dusting of hair upon his chest made her fingers itch to run her hands across his slick skin. He clasped his hands over his head as he bent from side to side to loosen his muscles but all Elysande could see was the warrior knight that was all Reynard. She marveled at his broad shoulders, his bulging arms, and all the way down to his strong well-toned legs… she licked her lips to moisten her suddenly dry mouth, not that 'twould do her much good. Seeing him thusly would remain etched in her mind until the end of time itself. She was completely lost.

Shaking herself out of the fantasy that raced through her head, she marched forward determined that Reynard would wear her favor this day. His smile when she neared reached his steel grey eyes, the edges crinkling in delight once she stood before him.

He bowed before her placing his hand over his heart. A courtly bow that would rival anything she had witnessed when paying homage to their empress. He towered over her when he finally stood tall, and he took her hand, raising it to his lips.

"Glad tidings to you this morn, *my* lady," he emphasized causing several nearby knights to swear.

"I thought I might miss seeing you this morn," she said stepping closer.

"I would not have begun my match without viewing your loveliness, Elysande," he said, and the baritone of his voice sent shivers racing over her suddenly hot skin.

"I have something for you… that is, if you would care to

wear it," she declared, holding out the blue and gold ribbon she spent the night working on.

He fingered the fabric. "You made this? For me?"

"Aye. To prove to all that you, above anyone else, are my champion," she said, smiling up into his face.

He held out his arm. "Then by all means, place your favor upon my arm. I am honored to receive such a gift, Elysande."

Taking the ribbon, she tied the favor above his bicep on his left arm. She stood back and gave him a deep curtsey. "May you be victorious this day, Sir Reynard," she said, beaming with pride. A trumpet blared, announcing the games were about to begin. "I best leave to find my place next to the empress."

"I will look forward to claiming all your dances this evening when I win the day," Reynard declared, giving her an appreciative look.

"Then I shall look forward to the evening meal," she whispered. Before she did the unthinkable and kissed the man in front of everyone, she left his side and hurried to take her place on the raised seating platform.

A brightly colored canopy flapped in the morning breeze. It had been erected to shield her from the glaring sunlight that would progress throughout the day. The empress was already seated with her ladies behind her. Only one vacant chair was placed next to the monarch. 'Twas specifically meant for Elysande so she would remain in the front for all to see.

"You are late," the empress stated with a look of displeasure etched upon her features.

"My apologies, Empress," Elysande replied whilst she bowed before her. The empress held out her hand, and Elysande kissed the empress's ring.

"Take a seat and let us see who shall take the lead in the quest to become the victor. There will be several days before a champion can be declared at the end of my games," Matilda declared. She waved her hand toward where Reynard and the men waited.

As the knights began to fill the center of the area, the empress stood. "My people… Welcome to my games," she said in a raised voice. A cheer rang out from those who were in attendance. "Over the next se'nnight, the knights before you will compete to not only keep you entertained but also to win Lady Elysande Thorburn of Blackmore's hand in marriage. Come the eve of each of those days, the knights who won their matches will dance with the lady and will advance to the next day at the games until only one remains her champion.

"Make no mistake, the winner and the lady *shall* be wed at the end of the games," she warned whilst her attention returned to the knights paying homage before her. "If any of you currently here before me have no plans to wed the fair lady, then excuse yourself now from these games." She waited to see if any of the knights would bow out. When none of the knights left the area, the empress motioned her hand toward the combatants. "Let the games begin!"

Another loud cheer rang out whilst a trumpet again blared, announcing the games were to begin. The knights took themselves to various areas of the field and began their matches. Yet, Elysande had her attention focused on Reynard. When his turn came up to begin to wrestle with another man unknown to her, she sucked in several deep breaths to calm herself. When he became momentarily pinned, she gasped whilst her fingers gripped the arms of her chair to the point that her knuckles became white.

"Someone please fetch Lady Elysande some wine," the empress ordered. A chalice was thrust toward her. She took the cup. "Honestly, my dear, how are you to survive an entire se'nnight if you cannot even sit still on the very first events?"

Elysande took a sip of her wine, declining the platter of fruit that was offered by another servant. "I only wish that you would have spoken to me before deciding a tournament would determine who my husband might be," she replied, her anxiety causing her to speak her mind with more frankness than perhaps was wise.

"You are a bold one this morn," the empress said, though thankfully she didn't appear to be particularly upset about it, clapping her hands when a man throwing a battle ax hit the target in its center. "I see Norwood wears what I assume is your favor."

"He is," Elysande declared, lifting her chin. If she were to be reprimanded for showing her preference so openly, then so be it. At least she would have had her say.

The chuckle that emitted from the empress surprised Elysande. She did not expect the woman to laugh at her plight. "I am not laughing *at* you, Lady Elysande," she said sternly before she continued. "Norwood is not... how should I put this... he is not as well established as the others who wish to wed with you. The early days of the conflict left his family with nothing. It is thanks to my good graces that his brothers have been restored to wealth and prosperity, but Reynard himself has nothing but the hope that I will bestow upon him lands and a title if he proves his worth. The competition will do him good."

Elysande could not reply to such a confession. All this because the empress wished for Reynard to prove himself to her? She would have thought he had already done so at the Battle of Lincoln and the latest siege at Winchester. What more could this woman want from one man?

⚜

CHAPTER NINETEEN

REYNARD STOOD IN the great hall, weighing his empty cup in his hand. He'd already drained it of its ale. Did he need another drink? Most likely not if he wished to keep his wits about him. 'Twould do no good to have his head pounding come the morn from indulging in too many spirits.

"I plan to rip that ribbon from your arm come the morrow, Norwood," a voice hissed beside him.

Lost in his thoughts, Reynard had not even heard the man's approach. "You can try, Morcant." He barely acknowledged the knight who was mayhap five years older than Reynard.

A grunt escaped the man. "I plan to do more than try. She was a fool to so obviously show where her affections lie. 'Tis like a beacon to every knight present to see who will be the first to take it from you."

Reynard glanced down at the dark blue ribbon with golden embroidery that he knew Elysande had slaved over. He had made the best attempt to launder the fabric since after only one day of wrestling matches, it had become soiled from when he'd rolled around in the dirt of the field.

"At least you all are aware whom she favors," Reynard said with a smirk, "and I will be the one who will wed with the lady." His gaze traveled to the dance floor where Elysande was finishing her dance with Lord Constantine.

"We shall see," Morcant muttered before a sly grin spread across his mouth. "In the meantime, I believe the next dance belongs to me. I will show you how a *man* handles a lady instead of what a mere boy is capable of."

Reynard lunged forward but was too late to grab a hold of Morcant's tunic. The knight gave a chuckle as he made his way to Elysande. Reynard could do nothing but watch from a distance when the pair went to begin the patterns of the next dance. He swore if Morcant's hand went any lower than Elysande's waist, Reynard would take great pleasure in removing his limb at the wrist.

"He only goads you, Norwood. Do not let him get the best of you," Warin drawled as though he had not a care in the world.

"Speaking from experience, Warin?" Reynard dared to ask. If anyone was competition for Elysande's hand, 'twas Constantine Warin. He was a favored knight with the empress and his estate was in close proximity of Oxford. What truly did Reynard have to offer his monarch besides the strength of his sword arm?

"If you cared to read the room, you would have noticed that Morcant has gone over to every single opponent this eve to goad and needle at them. His attempts to dig into my feelings for the lady and put me off the games come the morrow have been futile. But you are far younger than the rest of us so I suppose he thinks you are easier to manipulate."

"I have not been manipulated," grumbled Reynard and he thrust out his hand holding his empty tankard toward a servant who quickly filled his cup.

"If you say so, but by the looks of you I would say you are about ready to sever Morcant's head at the neck," laughed Warin. "Such an action might indeed be justifiable but mayhap you should not do something that vile during the evening meal."

"You know as well as I that the games are not to the death," Reynard answered whilst he continued to keep his eyes on Elysande.

"You and I may adhere to those rules, but others… perchance not so much. After all… the others are determined to win the tourney at any cost in order to win themselves a wife, her lands, and also the empress's favor." Warin continued to inspect Reynard and when he did not react he lifted his cup in a silent toast. "Keep it together, Norwood, and take out your frustrations at the game. Good eve to you."

Surprised that he seemingly had an ally of sorts with Warin, Reynard took several calming breaths. 'Twould do no good to cause a scene in front of the empress and as Warin said, he could take the matter up on the morrow on the field. He saw Hawke nod in Elysande's direction as her captain also keep close vigil over his charge. At least Reynard was not alone in his protectiveness with the woman. Now he only needed to survive the evening whilst watching Elysande dance with the victors of today's games. 'Twas going to be a long night.

ELYSANDE PUSHED ON the chest of the man who continued to pull their bodies far closer than the dance should have permitted.

"You will do well to remember you are under the close watch of… the empress," Elysande fumed but inwardly cursed herself when she realized she had about to utter Reynard's name. A hearty laugh was not what she expected to come pouring out from this man's mouth.

"I expect the empress is far too busy enjoying the evening's entertainment than to bother where I place my… hands," Gerold Morcant teased, pulling her forward so they were chest to chest. "You and I will be a fine-looking couple once we are wed."

"Looks are not everything, my lord. You will find that despite appearances, I am a very independent woman and not one to obediently sit in a solar with a bit of sewing whilst waiting for a man's return so I might serve him," she warned. The dangerous glint in his eyes caused her to halt anything further she might say, and she swallowed hard, feeling apprehensive.

"You can be anything you wish until we say our vows. After

that, you will always remain under my control," he snapped before he masked his features into something that Elysande supposed was to be pleasantness. If that was his objective, he failed for there was nothing pleasant about this man.

"You presume much. What makes you think you will win against the others who also fight for my hand?" she dared to ask.

"I will win because I need the victory more than any other," Gerold proclaimed with a forced smile. It must have galled him to admit he needed something from a mere woman.

"You mean you need my lands and whatever monies the empress will give me as a dowry," she hissed.

"Is there any other reason why I would take you to wife? You may be beautiful, Elysande, but so are a dozen other women here at court."

"Then marry one of them and leave me be," she ordered, attempting once more to place some distance from him without success.

"You will soon learn your place in my life. Until then, I do so enjoy a challenge. Now let us enjoy the rest of our dance together before the next man comes to claim you."

Mentally, she cursed this pompous *arse* to hell and back! But when she espied the empress watching closely, she forced her frown into a smile as though she was actually enjoying the moment of dancing with Gerold Morcant. Nothing could be farther from the truth.

The music thankfully died away and she quickly fled from Lord Gerold's side even whilst she heard his amused chuckle. How would she ever survive the next six evenings plastering a smile upon her face to appear as if she enjoyed herself? After only one night, she was already at her wits' end. Yet, what else could she do? The empress had made up her mind and the events that were to come needed to be played out for everyone's benefit but Elysande's.

As she left the middle of the dance floor, Hawke quickly came to her and thrust a chalice into her hand.

"You appear as though you are in need of a drink," he said calmly. "'Tis a good thing the dance ended. I was about to interrupt if that cur continued to manhandle you."

"I wish you would have, although I suppose such would not have gone over well with our empress. I wish this insanity was over and Reynard…" Her words trailed away and she swore she would not break down in tears at the prospect that she would be forced to wed another.

"You care for him." 'Twas a simple statement that spoke volumes.

"Aye."

"You could petition the empress and ask—"

"I tried without success. She seems bent on having Reynard prove to her his worth," she declared with a sob.

"Bah! Norwood has already done so or he would not be asked to accompany the empress whenever she travels. He is privy to the goings-on in the kingdom far more than most here," Hawke proclaimed, scowling.

"There are others who also are just as close to the empress. Richard Grancourt for one," she answered softly.

"Grancourt is not participating in the games. His readiness to serve the empress is not in question nor can he be numbered with the men who are attempting to win your hand," Hawke reminded her.

"Some of them are… obnoxious, to put it nicely," she replied and then took a sip of her wine. The liquid slid down her throat and hit her stomach reminding her she had barely supped this eve. She had been so upset at the prospect of what would happen tonight that she had given up earlier trying to swallow any food. If she was not careful, the wine would go straight to her head and then where would she be?

"You will come to me if any of them become too forward, Elysande. I care not what the empress says. I am still your captain and am sworn to protect you. I will not have you sullied by some overeager man bent on wedding you whether or not he wins the games. This includes Norwood. Do you understand me?" he asked, crossing his arms over his chest.

"Aye," she said before continuing, "but 'twill not come to that."

A lock of his blond-brown hair fell over his forehead and she reached up to push it back into place. She cupped his cheek but briefly before she returned her gaze back to the audience in the room. Everyone seemed to be watching her every move. It exhausted her to be on such public display.

The empress stood and the minstrels struck up a chord. Those in the great hall halted their conversations.

"Today's games have for the most part been a large success. As you all saw, several knights have been injured during the games and are no longer in the running for Lady Elysande's hand. On the morrow, we shall learn who will live to see the next day. But I will proclaim a champion for his efforts for this day. He shall have the pleasure of the last dance with Lady Elysande."

The empress began to survey the crowd and Elysande's eyes met Reynard's across the room. He gave a brief nod of his head and she returned the gesture before her attention returned to the empress. She held her breath waiting to hear Reynard's name…

"Lord Constantine Warin, Earl of Charlbury," the empress's voice rang out, causing several groans to be heard amongst the men even whilst Elysande's heart fell. "Come and claim your dance with the beautiful lady!"

Lord Constantine came to bow before the empress before his attention turned to find Elysande. When their eyes met and held, she swore all the color left her face whilst her gaze became unfocused. Elysande quickly turned, covering her mouth until she heard Hawke whisper in her ear to hold herself together. She squared her shoulders and placed another false smile on her lips hoping it at the very least appeared welcoming.

Lord Constantine came and lifted her hand high until they reached the middle of the vacant floor—no others would join them in the last dance of the evening. As the music began, she was expertly maneuvered through the patterns of the dance by a man who apparently knew how to court a lady. 'Twas a shame that this particular man was the wrong one for he would never be able to make her heart sing.

CHAPTER TWENTY

R AIN PELTED THE earth, turning the ground beneath his feet into a muddy trap and, yet, still the games went on. Reynard swung his sword at this opponent waiting for an opportunity to win the match. But Morcant was a challenging adversary and was not making it easy for Reynard to achieve his goal. But he refused to give up as he continued his assault.

His arm grew tired, not that he would allow such a weakness to cause him to fail. He drew on his inner strength that had previously seen him through sheer exhaustion when he was on a battlefield. There had been no time for weakness at Lincoln or Winchester and he would be damned if he would allow his body to fail him now! Not when everything depended on him being named Elysande's champion at the end of the games.

He shoved his helmet from his head when it became more of a hindrance than a help whilst the rain continued to restrict his eyesight. He had been certain the empress would cease the games for the day with such a torrential downpour but so far, she continued to applaud those who became victorious whilst she sat beneath a canopy that kept her and those who sat with her dry.

The wind suddenly whipped up causing one corner of the makeshift protection to fall. Water cascaded off to the side causing a river to form upon the ground. Reynard became distracted as he watched the empress and Elysande rush to stand. A piercing jab slid between the chinks of his chainmail beneath his tabard causing Reynard to fall in the mud to one knee.

"You should not let your emotions show so clearly on your face, Norwood. 'Twill be your downfall." Morcant sneered, lifting up his sword as he claimed the match.

Reynard regained his feet. Despite the wound that caused his side to burn, he would continue his fight with his foe. He swung his blade over and over again in a move that his brothers had taught him in their youth. No one in his past could handle such an onslaught as he continued to hack away at the man before him. His arm moved swiftly, and the action caught Morcant completely unaware considering he had thought Reynard was defeated. His eyes went wide when he stumbled and fell into the mud below Reynard's feet. Reynard pointed his blade at Morcant's neck.

"Yield," he ordered through the rain pounding on their bodies.

"Nay! I yield nothing to you or any other who thinks he is man enough to beat me," Morcant bellowed, rising up onto his elbows.

Reynard nicked Morcant's skin for emphasis. "The fact that my sword is at your neck is reason enough to end your fighting for the day. Yield," he repeated and waited for Morcant's reply.

"You bloody whoreson. Aye! I yield," Morcant swore and at last rose to his feet once Reynard pulled back his sword and placed the blade in the scabbard at his side. "Just remember what the morrow may bring. I will not yield again so easily."

Reynard gave a sigh of relief when he heard the empress announce that the games were at an end for the day due to the inclement weather. She began to descend from the raised platform along with Beatrix and her other ladies-in-waiting. Elysande's descent was slower as if she waited for him. He searched the ground for his helmet and once found, he picked it up and began to slowly make his way toward Elysande. He did not wish to alarm her but he must needs get to the tent he had had erected near the games in order to inspect the wound Morcant had inflicted.

He held his side until a quick look at his gauntlet confirmed his worst fears… the wound would most likely need stiches.

"You are bleeding," Elysande cried out as she took hold of his hand. She traced the metal gauntlet with her fingertips.

"So 'twould appear," he fumed, knowing Morcant would have been victorious if Reynard hadn't found the strength to carry on the match.

"Your tent is nearby?" she asked as she took his arm and placed it over her shoulder, as if this tiny woman would have the strength to keep him upright.

"Aye. Hopefully Blake, Oswin, Kingsley, or even Richard witnessed my injury and are already inside preparing what might be needed to treat the wound."

"The cur! Lord Gerold should be banned from any further participation," she complained angrily. "By the empress's edict, these games are not supposed to draw blood."

Reynard gazed down to look at the lady. Those blue orbs were filled with unshed tears as though his injury pained her. Bless her heart… "Not everyone plays by the rules, Elysande, no matter who makes them."

He led the way to his tent, fumbling with the rope holding the entrance closed. At last, it gave way and they were able to enter his humble dwelling. Since this was only a temporary place to rest his head during the games, there was not much inside. A pallet to lay down upon, a small table with a stool and a small fire that somehow had remained lit despite the constant sound of dripping water as it hit the embers from the opening above in the roof.

He plopped down on the stool and she quickly looked into the two pitchers placed on the table. One contained wine and the other water for washing that he had set out to be at the ready upon his return. She poured wine into a goblet and handed it to him. She found a cloth and brought the pitcher of water to the edge of the table.

"Let me help you get your chainmail off since your friends

have not made it here as yet," she offered taking the wine from his hands.

"You probably should not be here alone with me, especially given that I am about to disrobe," he said quietly even though he watched her every move intently.

"I have seen more of you during the wrestling matches than I see of you now."

A frown briefly formed on his brow, wondering if she had ever had to assist with bathing guests in her parents' household. It was a custom that usually went to the lady of the castle but Elysande had been managing on her own for who knows how long.

"And have you seen many men without their clothing?" he asked, only realizing after the words emerged that he had voiced his concerns aloud.

A snort left her. "Your wits must be addled from your injury to ask such a question."

He shrugged. "'Tis common enough in most cases."

Her eyes widened as though she suddenly figured out where his thoughts had taken him. She began yanking his tabard from his chest. "Do not allow such foolish notions to enter your mind, Reynard. And no… I did not perform such a function at Blackmore for any male guests that came to my keep."

Relief washed over him. When she bid him to lean forward, he did his best to oblige her orders. Once the heavy chainmail was removed, a gasp escaped her as she gently pulled at the padding that had protected his skin against the metal links.

"'Tis worse that I thought," she murmured as she lifted the linen to see beneath it. "Pull this off, too, so I can see how deep your wound truly is."

"Morcant knew where to inflict the injury without puncturing my lung." He grimaced when her fingers touched his skin.

"Lucky for you the scoundrel did not push any deeper or you and I might not be having this conversation," she replied with a frown between her brows. "I am going to need thread and a needle for this surely must be stitched."

Before another word could be spoken between them, Richard opened the flap of the tent. Reynard could only image what his friend was thinking, considering Elysande was kneeling between his legs whilst he was bare above the waist.

"What is going on here?" Richard asked stepping into the tent with Blake following close behind.

Elysande jumped to her feet whilst a becoming blush rushed across her cheeks. "Sir Reynard has been hurt and the wound will need stitches," she informed them, stepping out of the way when Richard came forward and began his own inspection of the wound.

Richard tossed Reynard a glare, and Reynard shot one back in return. His friend should have known Reynard did not have the strength to dally with a woman whilst a gaping hole was in his side. Richard looked up over his shoulder to Elysande. "The empress has asked for you in the great hall, Lady Elysande. Sir Blake will see you inside."

"But Reynard's wound," she began only for Richard to stand and take her hand, leading her toward the exit of the tent.

"I will personally see to the wound and ensure no fever sets in, my lady," Richard said coaxing a smile from Elysande's lips.

"You shall let me know if he becomes ill?" she asked full of concern.

"He will be well, my lady. Now go and attend our empress before she becomes impatient," Richard declared whilst he gave a nod to Blake to escort the lady back to the castle.

Once they left, Richard returned and took out the necessary items from his cloak to see to Reynard.

"I suppose 'tis best that I take care of this for you instead of your lady," Richard chided with a hint of censorship to his voice.

"Her needlework would have probably been... neater than what you are about to do to me," Reynard answered, reaching for his wine and taking a huge gulp. Once the needle entered his flesh, he grimaced and took another long pull. He would have preferred Elysande's gentle ministrations to what Richard was currently performing. At least then Reynard would have had someone pleasing to look upon.

CHAPTER TWENTY-ONE

T HE STORM CONTINUED to plummet down from the heavens for nigh unto two days. Elysande had heard Empress Matilda was in a foul mood because the weather was the reason the tourney could not continue. She had specifically planned the entertainment for a reason—actually, for several reasons, although finding Elysande a husband seemed secondary to keeping the empress's people happy during their time of strife. But the rain and the lack of events did not deter those who had traveled far to witness such an event. The empress's people continued to reside inside the castle, in tents pitched nearby, and filled the local inns in the village until such a time when the games could resume.

Elysande was left with time on her hands during the daylight hours. Since Reynard's injury, she had been forbidden to see him, causing her to become not only full of worry but agitated. That others were seeing to his injury plagued her when she wanted to be there for him herself. Surely someone who loved the man could care for him better than his comrades or even a knight who was like his brother.

She had sent Olive out earlier to see what she could learn about the seriousness of Reynard's illness. Servants tended to gossip. Elysande was certain that if any news was circulating within Oxford's walls, her maid would learn the truth of it. A knock upon her chamber door momentarily startled her out of her musings. Olive was returning faster than she expected.

After a call to enter, Olive opened the door and peeked her head inside to ensure they were alone. "He is now inside the castle, milady, in a bedchamber on the floor above you. They say Sir Reynard is ill with a fever and that the wound might be infected."

"And no one bothered to tell me," Elysande fumed whilst picking up the edges of her gown and heading toward the door. "Show me which room. I've had enough of waiting around like I am of no import. This man may become my husband, and I will no longer be treated like I do not have a say in his care."

Elysande marched down the passageway, up the circular turret stairs and down another long corridor until Olive pointed to a room. Kingsley was just leaving, and Elysande went up to him and attempted to see inside Reynard's bedchamber.

"How is he?" she asked when Kingsley blocked her view.

"A fever from the dirty blade. He should recover soon," Kingsley declared but he did not appear convincing.

"Richard was supposed to keep me informed," she announced stamping her foot upon the stone floor beneath her feet.

"Richard has been preoccupied with the demands of an angry empress. I doubt he has had any time to himself let alone to keep everyone informed about how Reynard is feeling," he said looking down upon her.

She pointed to the doorway. "I would think since Reynard is like a brother to Richard, that he would be concerned for his welfare."

"Aye! He *is* concerned but there is nothing more that can be done other than to wait for the fever to run its course. Richard has already shoved the doctor from this room when he wanted to bleed Reynard… like he has not already lost enough blood," Kingsley replied, running his hand over the back of his neck.

Elysande agreed with such an assessment. "I must needs see him."

Kingsley continued to bar her way into the room. "Sir Reynard is not at his best, my lady. You should wait for another day when he is better."

Her hands went to her hips. "Unless you wish to physically push me away from this room, then I must ask you to step aside, Kingsley," she answered, dropping any formality between them.

"But Lady Elysande—"

"You will not deter me from seeing Reynard. Now, please… move aside, Kingsley, so I can see for myself that I have no cause to worry for his life!"

Kingsley frowned but stepped out of the way, even going so far to open the portal wide so she could see Reynard laying upon his bed from the entrance to the bedchamber. But Elysande was not about to make her determination from the passageway. She stepped into the room. Kingsley made to follow but she took hold of the door and pushed hard on the wood.

"'Tis not seemly you should be alone with him," Kingsley said whilst even Olive's eyes went wide.

"What harm could possibly be done by a sleeping man?" Elysande argued, continuing to try to shut the door and slide the bolt into place.

"Much," Kingsley grumbled, "or else you do not know Norwood well after all."

"I will be fine," she interjected, giving the wood another push. She heard Kingsley curse before the door slammed shut. She did not hesitate to put the bolt in place.

Now that such unpleasantries were out of the way and she finally gained her purpose to see Reynard with her own eyes, she quickly rushed over to the bed. Beads of sweat covered his face and when she placed her fingertips upon his brow, she could feel for herself how hot his skin had become. A basin with water and a cloth stood on the small table next to the bed and she squeezed the excess water from the cloth and began to wipe his brow, his cheeks, and even his chest and arms. She dared not look any farther down than where the linen covered the lower half of his body and only concentrated on the task before her: cooling Reynard down so he might recover.

Minutes turned into hours and her back ached from leaning over his body, yet still she continued on with her ministrations. One moment he was hot, the next he would break out into a cold sweat, and during one of his bouts where he was overheated, he had thrown back the covers and Elysande got a clear view of his entire naked body. She had a moment of hesitation to appreciate the sight of what a fine-looking man he was. Yet in the next instant, she also thought that mayhap she was way over her head in thinking she could be the one to make him well. But she wrestled with the covers as he tossed and turned and finally was able to cover him once again. After this, she would be hard pressed to look at Reynard the same knowing she had seen him in all his glory!

At some point during the night, she had dozed off whilst resting her head on the bed next to him. She had awoken to the feel of his fingers playing with the tresses of her hair. She rubbed her eyes from her slumber and did her best to ascertain his condition. 'Twas difficult considering the only light was from the dying embers in the hearth.

"Elysande," he whispered so softly she could have easily missed him calling out her name.

"Reynard," she answered as she went to light a candle to place near his bedside to get a better view of him. Her hand reached out and she let out a sigh of relief when his skin felt normal to her touch. "Your fever broke."

"You should not be here," he protested as he cleared his throat and pulled at the linen to fully cover his chest.

"Aye, I should and would not allow others see to your care," she replied, pulling the stool closer to the head of the bed.

"What will people think? Especially the empress."

"I do not care what anyone thinks of me. Mayhap if they think I have taken advantage of you, then there would be no need for the games to continue," she teased, offering him a smile.

A grunt left him. "No one would believe such a tale."

Elysande shrugged and then noticed how ragged she must

appear. Her sleeves of her gown were rolled up to her elbows, her hair was most likely a tangled mess, and her gown was rumpled from sleeping on a stool. "I am glad you are better, Reynard."

He took her hand and raised it to his lips. "Thanks to you, my lady."

"I did not do much other than stay with you and try my best to break your fever," she replied with a blush. Now that he was coherent, she thought she had best take her leave.

"I still offer you my thanks. Now, I must beg you to take your leave and return to your own chamber. I will not have others think poorly of you."

"As you wish." She stood but hesitated to leave his side. She finally bent forward to place a quick kiss upon his lips before making a hasty retreat.

She leaned back upon the door once it closed behind her trying to catch her breath as the vision of Reynard's naked body refused to leave the memories etched in her mind. With fanciful thoughts flitting through her head, she began to make her way back to her own bedchamber to resume her slumber. If she had looked over her shoulder, she would have noticed Gerold Morcant frowning as he watched her leave Reynard's bedchamber.

CHAPTER TWENTY-TWO

REYNARD HAD MANAGED to make it to the great hall to break his fast once the new day had dawned, not that the sun was anywhere in sight. The storm continued to drench the land, making everyone irritable over being forced to stay indoors. If the empress's tourney had gone as planned, the games would now be over and Elysande would be his wife. He would not think of any other outcome despite the injury that had kept him in bed for two days.

Two days of other men vying for Elysande's attention, her conversation, or the opportunity to dine or dance with her. Two days of being laid low by the scum who also tried to put his claim upon her. He saw Morcant across the room speaking with the empress and watched the lady frown. By Saint Michael's wings… what nonsense was he filling the woman's ear with now?

Reynard rubbed his side even as he took another bite of the porridge he was attempting to consume. 'Twas hard to stomach anything this morn when the empress's court appeared to be filled with intrigue. What the bloody hell was going on? A nudge from Richard as he took a place next to him had Reynard pushing away the bowl.

"What have I missed in the two days I have spent recovering?" Reynard demanded and he once again surveyed the room. Was his imagination running amuck or was everyone staring at him?

"There is a rumor circulating this morn," Richard muttered,

tearing off a piece of bread and taking a bite.

"About what?" he asked, annoyed he was the center of attention.

"You."

"What have I done to earn their interest?" Reynard asked, curious why he was the topic of conversation when he had been abed for two days.

"'Tis not what you have necessarily done but who was seen leaving your bedchamber in the middle of the night," Richard replied, reaching for a piece of cheese. "The two of you should have been more careful about your midnight tryst."

A snort left Reynard. "'Twas hardly a tryst and you know it."

Richard shrugged. "Mayhap, but the point of the matter is Lady Elysande was *seen*. She may have been tending to your fever but in the eyes of those who wish to take your place, she is now sullied goods."

Reynard slammed his fist upon the table. "Do not call her such," he warned.

"There are several men who have already informed the empress that they are no longer interested in continuing in the games due to Elysande's current… situation."

Reynard's eyes flitted to the knight who continue to converse with the empress. "Does that include Morcant?"

A snarky laugh escaped Richard. "Ha! Not that one. If anything, he is more determined to have her despite what has transpired between you and the lady."

"I told you nothing happened."

"If you say so, but others will not be so easily convinced, *mon ami*," Richard said with a weak smile.

"So, the games will continue once the weather cooperates," Reynard suggested and watched Richard nod.

"I believe the empress is determined to give those who continue to grovel at her feet the entertainment she promised them."

"I can only pray the rain holds out for another day or two so I can recover fully," Reynard grumbled once more placing his hand over the wound.

"I think you have bigger issues to worry over than the weather, Reynard," Richard proclaimed with a nod of his head. "If you were not a target before, then you certainly will be now.

Reynard saw Elysande enter the great hall. She appeared radiant and he wanted nothing more than to proclaim to all present that she belonged to him. But the lords and ladies who were noticing her arrival began having conversations between them that were far from hushed. *Ruined. Tarnished.* Reynard scowled whilst he struggled to hold onto his temper as the name-calling reached his ears. This was what he had feared when Elysande left him last night.

Her entire visage lit up once she espied him. She was about to make her way in his direction when he gave a slight shake of his head. She halted her progress across the room and turned in the opposite direction to take a seat at another table to break her fast.

Reynard returned to his conversation with Richard. "I was a target the moment Elysande gave me her favor. Nothing will change that, and I shall continue to be honored to wear her ribbon."

"'Tis your neck you risk, but I warn you to watch your back. Morcant almost did you in. I would hate to have you lose your life over a woman. Wymar would have my own neck if any harm came to his youngest brother whilst under my watch," Richard retorted with cocky grin. "Not that you cannot take care of yourself."

"I shall deal with Morcant. I owe him," Reynard sneered. "Besides, no one told you to watch over me like I am some child. I would think you would find it of more import to keep your sister Beatrix out of trouble."

A sound of frustration left Richard's lips. "I swear she will be the death of me. She is flirting her way through the empress's court as if she, too, has no care for her reputation."

"She did warn you that she would do so when we left her here when we traveled to Bristol. Did you expect her to not follow through with her threat?" Reynard said with a laugh whilst he took a brief look at Richard's sister and Oswin talking together.

"Nay. She has never backed down to me in our past. 'Tis not in her nature to do so," Richard declared whilst he too watched his sister. "What do you think of what is going on with Oswin and Beatrix? Do you think he is in love with her?"

'Twas Reynard's turn to shrug. "Who is to say? Although if he was, would you object to the match? You already know the man and he is an honorable knight and more than worthy of her."

Richard ran his hand through his hair. "I never know what to think when the matter concerns Beatrix. However, I may need to interrupt their little interlude. Beatrix is taunting me by placing her hands on Oswin, and I would hate for our friendship to be ruined because my little sister is trying to make some point."

Richard excused himself and Reynard watched him cross the room. He leaned down to whisper in Beatrix's ear and quickly removed her from the hall. 'Twas clear Richard was about to reprimand his sister, though Reynard had the sense that rather than amending her behavior, she would only retaliate even more. He felt sorry for Richard knowing Beatrix would do all in her path to get her way... Reynard could only ponder if that included an alliance with Oswin Woodwarde.

CHAPTER TWENTY-THREE

ELYSANDE WATCHED AS Beatrix was whisked away from the room by her brother. She could only image what that conversation might be about since Richard had not appeared pleased. Beatrix, however, was not the only person who was being talked about since she could not miss her name being whispered among those she passed on her way to break her fast.

She had been so happy when she espied Reynard and would have joined him but when he shook his head to deter her, she could only wonder why he did not wish for her to eat with him. Then she became privy to the gossip that floated in the air. 'Twas about her! Someone had seen her leave Reynard's bedchamber last eve, but who?

Her attempts to eat the offerings before her were for naught since she all but choked on the food that passed her lips. She at last gave up and began looking around the room to determine who might have been the one to begin spreading the gossip among these shallow-minded people who only wished to gain the empress's favor. From the snide looks that were tossed her way, it could have been any number of men or women. Her eyes slid to Lord Constantine who raised his goblet toward her in a silent toast. He could be the culprit, but she had her doubts. Others gave her a wink as though they believed that now that she was ruined beyond repair, she would willingly welcome them into her bed. The cads!

Since she had no idea who to confront on spreading gossip,

she decided to make a hasty exit and return to her room. Better to hide away in the safety of her bedchamber than continue to be the topic of conversation that did not favor her.

She had barely closed the door, or so it seemed, before there was a knock. Thinking mayhap Reynard had decided to follow her, she opened the portal with a smile that quickly shrank from her face. She had not been expecting the entourage that stood in the passageway.

Surprise must have been reflected on her features as she saw the empress's attendants. Beatrix was also present and with a toss of her head entered first. The other three women followed behind her. Lady Eden Howlande, Lady Rovena Eatone, and Lady Petula Wintere were the empress's most trusted confidents. This could not bode well for Elysande.

"Ladies…" Elysande began as the women filled her chamber, finding various places to sit. "Is something amiss?" They all answered at the same time causing her eyes to widen.

"Everything is amiss," Petula started.

"Aye, unfortunately," Beatrix said smartly.

"'Tis of grave import," Eden replied, patting her hair into place, not that a single strand was out of place.

"Most definitely," exclaimed Rovena.

Since the available chairs were taken, Elysande was forced to stand as three of the four women inspected her as if looking for some flaw. "How may I be of service?" she finally asked.

Before any of them could answer, another knock sounded upon the door. 'Twas louder than when these women bid entrance, giving Elysande the notion that the person on the other side was impatient.

Elysande went to the door again and her mouth hung open before she quickly dropped down into a curtsey. She allowed the empress to enter, and Eden stood and vacated her seat. The empress began to drum her fingers on the arms of her chair.

"I am in a quandary where you are concerned, Lady Elysande," the empress stated.

Elysande came to kneel before her empress. "What can I do to please you, my Empress?" she quietly asked.

"What can you do to *please* me?" she repeated in a snarl of contempt. "You could have kept yourself from Norwood's chambers, to start with. What were you thinking? And to be caught by Gerold Morcant of all people. That man wasted no time spreading the word throughout my court to anyone who was willing to listen. I am surprised anyone is left who would continue to fight in my games to win your hand."

"Nothing happened," Elysande began to explain whilst a sound of disbelief left the empress's mouth.

"Nothing happened only because I was informed by Grancourt that Norwood was incapacitated with fever! Clearly you have had too much idle time on your hands since this infernal rain began," she snapped. She held out her hand until Petula went to Elysande's table to pour the empress a chalice of wine. Once she took a sip, she handed the cup back to her attendant.

"He slept the whole time," Elysande continued in her defense.

"And you were the only one who tended him which does not look good for you since clearly you are an unmarried young woman." The empress heaved a heavy sigh before she waved her hand for Elysande to at last rise to her feet. "I have come to the decision that you shall join my ladies in waiting and attend me as they do. That should keep you out of trouble long enough for the games to be completed."

"I am honored, my Empress," Elysande murmured, bowing her head to hide her true feelings of apprehension at being under the close scrutiny of her monarch.

"As you should be," the empress declared, coming to stand. "I shall expect you to be dressed accordingly. My ladies will ensure you have sufficient gowns and jewels to complete your attire for the evening meal."

The empress left as abruptly as she arrived whilst her ladies began to also exit from the room. Beatrix was the last whilst she held the handle of the door looking over her shoulder. "Do not worry, Elysande. 'Tis really not that bad to be an attendant for the empress."

"How often do you repeat such a mantra to yourself, Beatrix?" Elysande asked, already guessing what the answer would be.

Beatrix gave her a weak smile. "Almost every day…"

The door closed behind the young woman who was obviously not happy with her life. Elysande slumped back onto her bed once she was alone. Attendant to the empress, of all things… just when she thought her day could not get any worse now she would never have a free moment to be with Reynard.

When the time came for the evening meal, she was called to attend the empress to help her dress. The other women were familiar with the routine and Elysande could do little more than stay out of their way as they assisted the empress. Standing behind the woman during the meal until they were bid to finally eat was difficult considering all eyes were upon her. The evening lasted far into the night until Elysande was at last able to seek her slumber.

When the new day dawned cloudy but dry, Elysande knew that the games would once more begin. She had dismissed Olive after her maid had seen that she was gowned appropriately and that she was now ready to head down to join the empress and her ladies for the resumption of the tourney. She was just inspecting herself one last time to ensure all was in place with her attire when a sound upon her door interrupted her. Thinking one of the empress's ladies had come to escort her down to the hall to break her fast, Elysande gave no thought to inquire who was without. She automatically opened the door, expecting to see Beatrix or one of the other ladies-in-waiting.

Elysande had no time to call out for aid nor to even take a breath to scream as a cloth was quickly placed over her mouth and nose. With no choice, she breathed in a foul scent and began to lose her vision. The last thing she remembered was something heavy being thrown over her before she was hoisted like a sack of grain over a man's body. Then, she knew no more…

$$\text{---} \cdot \text{---} \cdot \text{---}$$

CHAPTER TWENTY-FOUR

REYNARD STOOD IN the middle of the tourney field with the few knights who were left to compete. The day remained cloudy, but the sun peeked out from the clouds on occasion. The empress had declared that her games would resume this morn and she was determined to see them through. The recent rains, however, caused the ground to remain wet from the rain whilst puddles of water had formed in several areas of the field. 'Twould make the mud beneath them treacherous, and Reynard could only hope he could keep his feet during today's matches. Now they only waited on the guest of honor. Elysande was late, and the empress voiced her displeasure.

"Where is she?" she demanded before turning toward a servant. "Find out what is keeping Lady Elysande so the games can begin.

The servant rushed off to do the empress's bidding whilst everyone else waited. The crowd that had been in attendance at the beginning of the games had now dwindled given the days the weather kept them away. Villagers had fields to till, lords had business matters of their estates to tend. Only those who were most determined to vie for the empress's favor remained… those who were willing to accept any meager offering from their monarch in return for their fealty.

Only half a dozen men were still eager to make Elysande their bride at any cost. Two were lesser lords in need of a wealthy heiress. Whilst Elysande had no ready funds, the dowry the empress had agreed upon was more than promising. One was a merchant hoping for a title and lands to call his own. Reynard glanced over to Warin and Morcant, the latter of whom had a smug look upon his face that only puzzled Reynard the more he stared at him. There was something going on with the man, but Reynard would take the matter out upon the field of honor.

Several more minutes passed when the servant returned with Elysande's sobbing maid. The empress bid the men who awaited the games forward.

"It appears that Lady Elysande has either fled Oxford or something afoul is afoot. I present a new challenge to those of you who are left to fight," the empress said with a scowl. "The one who finds her shall win the privilege of her hand."

"Bloody hell," Reynard cursed, watching the men take off at a run. But leaving without learning any further information was futile and he decided to see what else Olive might be privy to. Lord Constantine came abreast of him, clearly of the same mind, whilst Hawke ran in their direction.

"She would not just take off and flee to possibly incur the empress's wrath," Hawke declared, looking over to Reynard.

"Are you certain? Perchance she did not like the direction the games were heading," Warin said whilst his gaze went to the crowd.

"I agree with Hawke, especially when she knows what is at stake," Reynard replied as they picked up their pace.

"She favors you still," Warin replied although he did not appear as though this bothered him overly much.

"Then why were you still willing to compete in the games?" Reynard inquired with a raised brow.

A snort escaped the knight. "Mayhap call it morbid curiosity to see if I could get her to find some small measure of a common accord between us."

"And have you thus far?" Reynard could not help but ask.

A sound escaped him. "Not particularly," he muttered beneath his breath. "The matter has become a matter of manly pride, I suppose. To see if I would be the last man standing. You understand, of course."

"Aye… of course," Reynard said, hating that he was agreeing with a rival for Elysande's hand.

"Her maid may know more than she thinks. 'Twould bode well to see if we can learn anything from her," Warin continued.

"Another thing we can agree upon. If this keeps up, we may end up as friends," Reynard said with a laugh although the situation was nothing to be merry about.

A grunt escaped Constantine. "I would not go *that* far, Norwood, but we shall see."

But Olive did not have any words of wisdom to impart to the pair. Nay. The only information she could tell them was she had attended Elysande this morn nigh unto two hours ago as she prepared to go down to the hall to break her fast before the games began. If someone had abducted the lady, then they most likely had a two-hour head start to wherever they would take her.

Hawke cursed. "Who would be so bold as to take the lady?"

Reynard rocked back on his heels. "I may have a notion."

"Well? Out with it, man. Who do you think abducted Lady Elysande?" Constantine bellowed.

"Morcant," Reynard said, planting his feet wide.

"He is not that big of a fool," Constantine said, shaking his head.

"You think not? Perchance you did not observe him whilst we were waiting for the tourney to begin. He had a smugness upon his visage that spoke to the idea that he knew something was up. He may not have taken her himself, but my guess is he had something to do with Elysande's disappearance."

"Hiring someone to do the deed *is* more his style than dirtying his own hands with the deed. I daresay he would have her removed to his territory—his lands are to the east near Stevenage," Constantine stated as he pulled his tabard over his chest.

"'Tis north of London?" Hawke asked, following Reynard who headed in the direction of his tent.

"Aye," Constantine answered before continuing. "I suggest we saddle our horses and ride together in that direction to rescue the lady."

Reynard halted his progress. "You must know I will not allow anyone other than myself to wed Elysande."

An unexpected chuckle left Constantine. "Then we best ensure we find her first so you can marry the lady."

"You are willing to give me aid?" Reynard asked, surprised the man before him would give in that easily.

"If I cannot convince her that we would suit, then I will concede the matter. However, do not blame me if I give it my best effort once we find her."

Somehow finding an ally with Lord Constantine was almost a miracle but he would take whatever help he could find. Although another argument ensued, Reynard convinced Hawke to stay behind in the event Elysande was returned. When Reynard caught up with Oswin, Blake, and Kingsley, they, too, agreed to accompany him. Richard, however, had his hands full in his attempts to tame his sister. For now, time was of the essence, and Reynard could only hope that Elysande had not come to any harm.

CHAPTER TWENTY-FIVE

E LYSANDE PEERED INTO the darkness of an unknown room. When she had awoken from her drugged state, she had found herself gagged, with her limbs tied onto the arms and legs of a wooden chair. Frantic to free herself, she fidgeted in her attempts to loosen the ropes but that only caused the chair to tip over. She would have screamed in outrage if she had been able. Her hands were cramped, and her side ached from her current position.

How many hours she laid tied to the chair upon the wooden floor, unable to right herself, she could not say. When the door to her prison at last opened, the sounds of voices in the distance confirmed she was in a room at an inn. Which one and where, she could not say. But that mattered little at the moment whilst she silently glared at the man who entered. His laughter only grated on her already frayed nerves.

"My, my," he cooed coming to squat before her. He took one fingertip and tapped her nose playfully. "You seem to be in a bit of a predicament, are you not, my lady?"

He took hold of the frame of the chair and easily lifted her back up so she was finally sitting up straight. She swore all the blood ran from her face once she was finally upright. He went back to the door, and someone handed him a tray. He held the platter with one hand, closing the door with the other and putting the bolt in place. He set a platter of food before her on the table, and her mouth watered at the heavenly fragrance of a meal. How long had it been since she had eaten?

He went to the hearth and built up the fire. She heard more than saw him fidgeting with something whilst out of her vision. He came back to the table with a candle. The room, now well lit, did little to give her any sense of comfort. "Run down" came to mind as her eyes glanced at the worn coverings on the bed.

Morcant demanded her attention when he waved a knife in front of her face. Obviously, he wanted her for something, so she did not think he meant to kill her. If that had been his objective, she would already be dead on the side of the road.

"If you promise me you will not call out, I will loosen your hands and remove your gag. If not, you can starve for all I care. Do we have an agreement?"

Her stomach rumbled in protest, causing him to chuckle again. Elysande could only nod her head for an answer. When her hands were freed, she rubbed at her raw wrists. The gag came next, and she greedily reached for the tankard that had been set on the table. The ale was warm but she did not care. Her only thought was that the brew quenched her parched mouth. Once she had drunken her fill, her glare returned to her captor with all the hatred she could muster inside her whilst her legs continued to be restrained at her ankles.

"What is the meaning of this, Morcant?" she finally asked when she found her voice.

"'Tis not obvious to you?" he returned with a sly grin.

"Nay, 'tis not obvious, you fool," she answered before she began to partake of the meal before her. He may be her enemy, but she would at the very least eat her fill before he decided to be less than civil and take it away.

Morcant shrugged, leaning back in his chair and folding his arms over his massive chest. He was a mountain of a man with brown hair and eyes so dark they were almost black. In her mind, she likened him to the devil.

He continued to watch her eat as though he was trying to determine how much he would tell her. His deep voice filled every corner of the room as he made his confession. "I was going to lose. I saw no reason why I should not take advantage of the situation and steal you away so you would have no choice but to become my bride."

"I will never be your wife," she warned whilst she quickly reached across the table for the knife he had set down. But he was quicker and snatched the blade away, putting it in his belt.

"Tsk, tsk, my dear. I thought we had come to an agreement."

"Aye… I agreed not to call out so I could partake of this food. I have not done so. I gave no promise that I would not try to kill you if the opportunity presented itself," she said, eyeing him warily.

"Is that any way to behave toward your future husband?" he said in such a mockingly sweet tone it made Elysande want to retch.

"I will never willingly agree to become your wife, Morcant," she snapped whilst she held back angry tears threatening to run down her cheeks. She took another bite of food.

A frown marred his brow before he rose from his chair. He pushed the plate away from her and then quickly replaced the linen in her mouth to prevent her from replying or making any attempt to call out for help. He then quickly retied her hands to the chair. She was once again immobile and could do nothing more than wish him dead.

He hovered over her. There was no place she could move to distance herself from him. "Whether you willingly say your vows is of little concern to me. We will wed once we reach my home near Stevenage. My priest will be more than happy to wed us once he learns you have been compromised. He will think he is doing us a favor by saving our souls."

His smug expression gave the impression that he had thought of everything but Elysande knew one thing he had not most likely not thought of. Reynard would move heaven and earth to find her.

Morcant took up the tray, gave her a wink, and left. She

would have cried out in frustration but what good would that do her? She needed some sort of a plan but there was little hope of escape considering she was tied to a chair. She would need to wait and try to be patient. Morcant's guard would slip at some point, or so she prayed.

His return mayhap an hour later caused her own guard to go up. He weaved his way into the room unsteadily, clearly having drunk his fill down below in the tavern. He untied her hands and feet and for one fleeting moment, she thought this might be her chance. He pulled her against him whilst arms of steel wrapped around her waist.

"Take care of your…*needs,* and do not let me regret loosening your bonds," he said quietly nodding to a corner of the room where a chamber pot was at the ready. 'Twas a grim reminder that she had not used a necessary since before the time of her capture.

Of course, 'twould be located furthest from the door, but her need was great, and she was well aware she must take advantage of what he offered in case he changed his mind. But how was she to see to her private matters when he watched her so intently?

As if he had come to some decision to trust her, Morcant went to the window and opened it before he began to lower his hose and braies enough to relieve himself. She gasped that he would be so brazen and another chuckle left him.

"You best hurry before I finish," he ordered. She knew if she were to take care of her own needs with any kind of privacy, then she best hurry before she had an audience.

Since he was preoccupied with his own business and his back was turned away from her, Elysande rushed across the room. She looked over her shoulder to see if he would watch her but his attention still appeared as though he was engrossed in the view out the window. She quickly took care of her own issues that had gone unattended. When she finished, she stood and took a step toward the door. The window slammed shut and he crossed the room so fast she barely had time to whirl away from the brute who took hold of her wounded wrist. She hissed when his fingers dug into her raw flesh.

He frowned before he lifted her hand to inspect the injury. He pulled her over to a wash basin and nodded toward the pitcher of water and the drying cloth. He turned away from her once more and sat on the edge of the bed. He removed his boots and the heavy sound of them hitting the floor caused Elysande to jump.

She continued to clean her wrists and wash her face before she took the cloth to dry herself. She heard the sound of a buckle being released and she took a short glance to see that he had placed his scabbard holding his sword at the head of the bed. If only she had the strength to lift such a blade—but she knew there was no way she was capable of such a deed. She was all but finished when Morcant pulled his tunic over his head.

Once again, she turned her back to the man but not before she caught a glimpse of him. There was no doubt he was a handsome man but therein lay the problem. He knew he was good-looking.

"Do you like what you see, Elysande?" he whispered when he came to her, pulling her back into his chest.

"Go to hell, Morcant," she swore only to feel herself pressed firmly into his body. Good heavens! He was aroused, and he made no effort to hide his desire.

"A pity you are unwilling this eve, but we will have a lifetime to become intimate," he said in a husky whisper. He reached around her to gather the cloth she had used, and he began tearing the linen into strips. He went to the bed and patted the mattress. "Come here."

Her eyes went wide. "I think not!"

"Did you think that was a request?"

"I am not sleeping in that bed with you," she complained, hugging her arms around her.

"And I will not wake come the morn to find you are gone. Now, come here!"

She refused to budge and Morcant took matters into his own hand, stood, and dragged her over to the bed. She opened her mouth to scream but found her mouth was the first to be bound. Her wrists came next but at least it was linen instead of the coarse rope that had already caused her wrists to bleed. But any thoughts of not having to deal with the rope quickly fled when Morcant tied the two of them together. He lifted her so she was on the side closest to the wall. If she'd had any hopes of escaping, they were gone. She would have to climb over him even if she were able to get free of the ties that held them far closer together than she would have wished.

"Sleep well, bride-to-be," he said before he placed a quick kiss upon her lips.

She could only glare at him and in her mind curse him to hell and back. When soft snores came to the man lying next to her, she began to relax knowing he would not take her maidenhead. She was safe… at least for this eve. And as she closed her eyes to find her own slumber, she began to pray that Reynard would be close come the morn. She needed him more than ever. Surely God would answer her prayers.

CHAPTER TWENTY-SIX

R EYNARD WAS IN a foul mood. When they had set out yesterday morning, he had been certain they would have caught up with Morcant by now and Elysande would now be safe. But that had not proven to be the case. After a cold night sleeping on the ground and with a new day dawning, he was perplexed on how they might have missed them.

"Would he have spent the night at an inn?" Oswin asked as they all stared at the empty road ahead of them.

Constantine snorted. "'Twould be just like his arrogance to think he was safe from pursuit and do so."

Reynard cursed. "We are too far east and clearly have missed them somewhere on the road." He leaned an arm on the pommel of his saddle before he paused in his musing to look over his shoulder. "Was there not an inn mayhap around five miles back?"

Blake nodded. "Aye. I believe you are right. We should have stopped to see if Morcant or any of his men were there."

Reynard pulled the reins of his horse to turn the steed around. "'Twas a stupid move on my part. I was blinded to all else but the thought that Morcant would head directly home."

Kingsley pulled his horse forward. "Who knew Morcant would be that overconfident to think he could so easily avoid a confrontation and spend the night in comfort?"

Constantine pulled at the neck of his cloak. "We all should have thought of such a happening," he snapped. "Now we have wasted precious time and have to backtrack."

They put their horses into a gallop and returned the way they had come. There was no one on the road except a farmer hauling a wagon piled high with hay. Only once they were in the courtyard of the inn did they halt their steeds. Scanning the area, they espied one of Morcant's men entering the stable.

Reynard could only assume that Morcant was inside since there was not a horse to be seen ready to leave the yard. They tied the reins of their horses to a post and entered the inn. The tavern was only half full and Morcant sat at a table with a couple of other men breaking his fast.

"Norwood! Warin!" Morcant called out. "'Tis a surprise to see you here, but come join me and eat your fill."

Reynard spoke over his shoulder to his friends. "Scan the rooms and anywhere else Elysande might be kept."

Blake, Oswin, and Kingsley took off in separate directions whilst Reynard and Constantine approached Morcant. That Elysande was not with him caused Reynard's anger to surge.

He came to the table and banged his fist on it, causing the platters and goblets to rattle on the wood. "Where the bloody hell is she?" he demanded, wanting to wipe away the smirk that swept across Morcant's mouth.

He put up a front of indifference, holding up his hands as if to say he would not pick a fight. "Where is who? As you can see, I am only breaking my fast with my men."

"You damn well know who I am talking about," Reynard bellowed. "Where is Lady Elysande?"

Morcant's eyes widened as though in surprise. "Lady Elysande is missing?"

"You are perfectly aware she is missing since you were there when the empress demanded we find her." Reynard lurched across the table before Constantine pulled him back and placed his hand on Reynard's shoulder, reminding him to calm down. 'Twould do no good to instigate a fight in the confines of a tavern.

"You best reveal where you are hiding her, Morcant," Constantine warned with a glare. "The empress will not stand for having one of her ladies abducted right under her nose."

Morcant waved his hand in the air. "Search the place, if you like. I have no idea what you are talking about for I have not abducted anyone." He went back to eating his meal as if he did not have a care as to what they did or who was missing.

His friends returned several minutes later but Elysande could not be found. They took their conversation outside so Morcant would not overhear their discussion.

"Thoughts?" Constantine asked the men as they stood in a circle.

Oswin ran his hand on the back of his neck. "We certainly cannot force the issue with Morcant if we do not have the lady as a witness. Only she can say who took her from Oxford."

Reynard began pacing back and forth in thought. "I know in my gut he took her…"

"We have no proof," Kingsley reminded him.

"Aye. We cannot accuse him of kidnapping the lady if the lady is nowhere near him," Blake added with a frown.

Reynard suddenly looked up, then turned his attention to the road. What if… "The farmer with the cart!"

"You mean to say you think we rode right past her? Morcant hid her in the cart?" Constantine growled.

Reynard waved his hand and the men went to their horses. "Think about it," he proclaimed as he vaulted into the saddle. "'Tis the perfect escape. He had to have known we would come in pursuit, so he puts himself in plain sight even as he hides the lady in a pile of hay. We find him sitting idly by at an inn filling his belly, and we are forced to admit that the lady is not with him. All the while, his captive gets closer to the security of his gates where escaping will be more difficult. It makes sense."

The men agreed and once more they were galloping down the road. Could finding Elysande really be as simple as catching up with a wagon? There was only one way to find out. The faster they traversed the miles between them, the closer Reynard came to having Elysande back in his arms.

Time ticked away and held little meaning much like the constant waves that swept over the shore. Reynard was once again impatient and on edge as he scanned ahead for signs of the cart.

And then, just as the road curved to the right, the last image of the back of the wagon caused Reynard to slap the reins, causing his horse to bolt forward. He called out a warning to the driver who suddenly saw that a group was pursuing him. He, too, slapped the leather straps to the horse that pulled the cart, but whilst the horse did its best to pick up its pace, the old farm horse 'twas no match for men on battle steeds.

Blake rode ahead, halting the horse. The driver of the cart pulled out a sword from the floorboard and held the blade forward.

"You will not rob me," he said as if this was their intent.

"Nay, we shall not take any goods that are rightfully yours. But we believe you have something that does not belong to you," Oswin sneered, holding out his own sword. From his height advantage, the driver of the cart dropped his blade whilst Reynard jumped from his horse and carefully entered the cart from the rear. He began fumbling around, moving the hay when he at last heard her muffled cries.

Tossing hay from the wagon, he began inspecting every inch of the bed of the cart. He finally found Elysande, tied and gagged, buried beneath the weight of the hay. Blue eyes swimming with unshed tears gazed at him in happiness. The first thing he did was untie the linen from her mouth.

"Reynard," she sobbed. "I knew you would come for me."

Working on the knots at her wrist, he finally decided to slit the ropes and drew a knife from his belt. "I will always find you, Elysande."

With the ropes cut at her wrists and feet, she flung her arms around his neck whilst crying into his shoulder. "I was so scared."

He held her close, caressing her hair as he tried to soothe her worries. "Shhh, Elysande. I have you now."

Once she had cried enough that the shoulder of his tunic was soaked, Reynard helped her from the cart but continued to hold her close. There was no way she was leaving his arms.

Constantine came and gave her a short bow. "My lady," he began. "I am pleased to see that overall you are well."

"Lord Constantine," she replied in surprise. "You are the last person I expected to come to my aid."

Constantine shrugged. "We were headed in the same direction so I thought I would join Norwood and his friends on a little adventure."

Reynard gave a grunt of displeasure. "A little adventure? Is that what we are calling this?"

"The lady is well and now in good hands." Constantine pointed to Elysande's raw wrists. "Name the whoreson who took you from Oxford and visited these indignities upon you."

"The one who captured me from my chambers was unknown to me. I only caught a glimpse of him before he put a cloth dosed in something over my face. I passed out cold once I was hoisted over his shoulder," she replied, putting her arm around Reynard's waist.

"And then…" Reynard urged her to continue.

"The next thing I knew I woke up in some rundown inn tied to a chair. I was alone until Gerold Morcant strode into the room," she answered softly. "He taunted me with his plans to force me to marry him."

"'Tis clear he was behind the whole plot to take you. The rat bastard!" Oswin snapped.

Blake's hand covered the hilt of his sword. "He has no honor. We need to head back to the inn and take him into custody."

Elysande began to tremble in Reynard's arms. "I cannot face him again," she pleaded, looking up into Reynard's face.

Constantine stepped forward. "I believe the last thing Lady Elysande needs is to face her abductor at this time. Do you not agree, Norwood?"

Reynard pulled Elysande closer and kissed the top of her

head. "Aye. I agree. I will take Elysande and quickly return her to Oxford. You and the rest of the men can head back to capture Morcant. I'm certain he is still probably eating his fill thinking he is safe."

Kingsley frowned. "And who will watch your back whilst you travel? Richard will kill us if anything should happen to you."

Reynard lifted Elysande onto his horse and then put his foot in the stirrups. He adjusted her so she was sitting on his lap, given that he didn't have a pillion to put on the rump of the horse, and he refused to have her further injured by riding without the extra cushion. Besides, he liked having her as close as possible.

"I will be careful. 'Twill not be the first time I ride alone. If you all are capturing Morcant and ensuring he does not make any more trouble, then Elysande and I will be perfectly safe."

His friends protested and argued whilst Constantine only had a grin upon his face. In the end, Reynard and Elysande left on their own and put the road behind them as they trotted off toward Oxford. Reynard was more than happy to have Elysande to himself with no one else vying for her attention.

CHAPTER TWENTY-SEVEN

ELYSANDE SNUGGLED CLOSER to the warm body that held her close. The steady gait of the horse beneath them had gently rocked her into a slumber a short while ago. 'Twas only when the beast began to slow that she awoke. She peered into the darkening sky, knowing they would never arrive at Oxford before the gates were closed for the evening.

Reynard adjusted his cloak around her, and she clung to his body as though he was everything she needed to support her after her ordeal with Morcant. And he was… He had saved her just as she knew in her heart that he would. A smile formed on her face knowing she was safe in his arms.

"We shall have to spend the night either in the woods or in a nearby inn if you can manage more time in the saddle," he murmured softly.

"I do not care where we rest our heads as long as I am with you," she said playing with the edges of his dark brown hair.

"I doubt you would appreciate nothing more than my cloak and a pallet against the ground, Elysande."

"You will be here with me… as I just said, I care not if I am laying on a bed of rocks as long as I have you."

A chuckle left him. "I am certain I can find you a better bed than a pile of rocks. I believe there is an inn perchance another mile up the road. Can you make it that far?"

"Aye," she declared happily. "I could travel to the ends of the earth with you, Reynard, and never tire of the journey."

He lifted his chin off the top of her head to place a kiss there instead. "You are a marvel, my lady. Hold tight," he said as he kicked his heels into the side of his horse, urging it to pick up its pace so they might arrive sooner rather than later.

Elysande tightened her hand around his waist and returned her head to his shoulder. If there had ever been a person made for another then 'twas Reynard for her. True… there was still much for them to learn about one another but they had a lifetime for that once they were wed. She had no doubt the moment they returned to Oxford Castle, the empress would be calling for her priest. They would not have to wait to marry, especially not after spending the night alone together.

The sun had set by the time they arrived at the inn. 'Twas in better condition than the last one, from what she could tell. Yet there was still loud male laughter coming from the common room. The sound of it caused her to quake. She tried to calm her racing heart for surely she was made of sterner stuff and Reynard would protect her.

A lad came from the stables, and after Reynard jumped down, he handed the boy the reins. Turning back to Elysande, Reynard raised his hands toward her. She lifted her one leg over the pommel and placed her own hands on those broad shoulders. She slowly slid down his body much like she did when they had danced together. Tingling warmth spread through her, and her only thought was how much she wished for him to kiss her.

But her feet touched the ground, and the moment was gone, at least for now. Reynard went to his saddle and untied the satchel that hung there, tossed it over his shoulder and then took her hand.

He called over his shoulder to the boy. "Take could care of my horse and see that he's well fed."

"Aye, milord," the boy replied as he led the steed in the direction of the stable.

Reynard went to open the door. "Stay close."

Elysande could only nod before everything seemed to hit her

at once. The smell of food, the warmth from a blazing hearth, being here with Reynard were all pleasant sensations, but there were other emotions that hit her too as they moved into the main room of the tavern. Unknown male voices who briefly halted their conversations to stare at them. Inspections from those closest who looked as though they would strip her gown from her in a moment if they could but reach her.

One drunk began to weave his way through the crowded room. "How much to spend an hour with yer woman?" he slurred.

Reynard pushed Elysande behind him. "Back off if you wish to see another day. This lady is my wife," he ordered, watching the drunk put up his hands in surrender and then grab the bottom of a serving maid who passed him by.

Elysande clung to the fabric on Reynard's back until she felt him relax, knowing they would not be accosted by any other fools.

"We need a room for the night," Reynard said to the man behind the bar. He went to the pouch at his belt and took out several coins. "A bath for my wife would also be appreciated.

"Up the stairs, fourth door on the left, milord. I'll have a tub brought up as soon as the water is heated," the man answered, calling out toward the kitchen to relay the request.

Reynard pushed Elysande ahead of him as they went up the stairs. No one followed them and soon they entered the bedchamber. She quickly inspected the room. The bolt at least in this room would hold. A screen sat in a corner and she assumed a chamber pot was there for their convenience. There was kindling and firewood sitting next to the hearth and as soon as Reynard set his satchel down, he went to build up the fire where only bright red embers were still burning.

"I know 'tis unseemly that we should spend the night together in one room but I thought 'twas best to keep up the appearance that we are wed. 'Tis safer that way," he said coming to a stand.

Elysande wrapped her arms around herself. "I will most likely need some time to adjust to not feeling like everyone is watching me like a prize for the taking. First the tournament, then Morcant, and now down below." She shuddered.

He came to her, taking her cheeks in his hands and bending forward to place a chaste kiss upon her lips. "I will not allow anything or any person to ever harm you again, Elysande, and that includes myself. Surely you know that."

She raised a hand to brush her fingertips over his own stubbled cheek. The shadow that had grown throughout the day was almost as black as the midnight sky. "Aye… I know I am safe with you."

He nodded and would have said more but a knock came at the door. Several servants began filling the room. Two men brought in a large wooden tub big enough for two whilst several more filed in bringing buckets of water and began to fill said tub. They set the extra pails for rinsing near the hearth to keep warm. They left just as quickly but not before several women entered with enough food and wine for the empress's entire army.

Once everyone was gone, there was an awkward silence until Reynard went to take the screen and place it in front of the tub to ensure her privacy.

"Your bath awaits you, my lady," he said motioning for her to enjoy this bit of luxury. "Best hurry before the water grows cold."

"But dinner—"

"—will be waiting for you once you are finished."

She took a hesitant step toward him. Could she dare ask him to… she could not even finish the sentence in her head so how would she voice it aloud?

"You and I will be married once we return to the empress," she stated as a fact and inwardly sighed in relief when he nodded his head and took her hand, bringing it to his lips.

"Aye. As soon as the priest can be called, 'tis my plan. And from your words 'tis your intent as well." His deep baritone voice sent shivers down her body, causing a warm blush to rush across her fevered skin.

"Aye, 'tis my fondest wish. You would have been my choice in a husband without the games," she declared stepping even closer.

"I do not know if the empress will reward me any monies that will help you restore Blackmore let alone add to your estate's wealth," he said with a frown.

She reached up to smooth the crease in his forehead. "I care not what monies you bring to *our* coffers."

"Your parents will think I wed you only for your land and any wealth the empress bestows upon you," he continued, appearing uneasy.

"I know better. Besides, Blackmore will be ours, together. My parents never cared for the place. It belonged to my grandfather, and he always told me it would belong to me once he was gone. My parents preferred our lands in Normandy, so they had no issue of letting me run the place when my grandfather began to age."

"I still do not see what advantage our marriage will benefit you. I am but a lowly knight in service to our empress," he admitted, showing his weakness.

A light laugh left her, causing the edges of his mouth to lift. "What advantage?" she said merrily. "Why, I will have you, my dearest Reynard. That in itself is the biggest reward I could ever have."

"You are like a bright star lightening up my life, Elysande," he murmured, taking her in his arms.

The sentiment warmed her heart and gave her the courage to state aloud the early unfinished thoughts that had swept into her mind. "That is why I propose we share the tub. 'Tis big enough for two and we can pull the table over to the edge and sup whilst we bathe."

His eyes widened at her proposal before a chuckle escaped him. "You must think I am a saint if you think I can disrobe, get into a tub with you, and then not make you mine in every way."

She pulled at the edge of his tunic until the linen went over his head. She looked her fill and she could not help herself from skimming her hands over his furred chest. Her fingers tingled at the contact.

"Then let our lives together begin this night for I have no intention of leaving this room a virgin. If nothing else, the deed will be done, and the empress cannot change her mind as to who I will marry."

"You seem to have thought this all out."

"I have had plenty of time to think *everything* out whilst I was tied up for the last two days. There is no sense in you waiting for me to complete my bath, not when we can accomplish two things at the same time. That is… unless you do not want to join me." She hid her smile as she moved the screen that had been intended to shield her from his view. There was no need for it now if Reynard was to join her.

A hoarse croak sounded and she looked over her shoulder to see for herself that he wanted her as much as she wanted him. The evidence? The bulge clearly outlined under his hose now that he no longer wore his tunic.

"I would have to be insane not to wish to join you, Elysande."

She nodded. "Help me pull the table over," she ordered quietly and together they moved their feast so it would be within reach whilst they soaked in the tub.

She had no regrets as she stripped her soiled garments from her body, nor could she miss the hungry look upon the face of the man she loved. He watched her every move and she could only pray that outwardly she appeared like she knew what she was doing in the art of seduction. Inside she was terrified she would disappoint him once he took her to bed.

CHAPTER TWENTY-EIGHT

R EYNARD SWALLOWED HARD as he watched Elysande raise her leg to test the water before she slid her luscious, naked body into the tub. Knowing that she waited for him to join him made the tingling sensations in his own body grip like a vise. He had never ached for a woman this much in his life. Mentally he tried to calculate when the last time was he had taken one. Far too long, but that was not the reason for this intense hunger. None of the women from his past meant anything to him. They were frivolous encounters to satisfy his basic needs with the exception of Johanna.

He let the memory of a woman he had loved slip aside. She no longer had a place among the living. There was only one lady he wished to ever take to his bed again and she beckoned to him with a crook of her finger like a breath of fresh air. He would not let her wait any longer.

His boots thudded on the wooden floor beneath his feet as each one was removed. Reynard watched Elysande carefully whilst she took a sip of her wine. She appeared so confident whilst watching him begin to remove his hose, but he knew 'twas just a façade when her hand shook returning the chalice to the table. When his braies came next and he stood before her in nothing but what God had granted him, her eyes widened. Reynard held back a smile. She may look the seductress but there was no doubt Elysande was a maiden just as she claimed.

A virgin… once again, his mind slipped into his past. He had never taken a woman who was not already experienced. He would tread slowly for he did not wish for her first encounter with him to be anything but pleasant after the initial act of claiming her maidenhead.

He went to the opposite side of the tub and lowered himself into the warm water that sloshed over the rim. A light laugh came from the lady who moved her legs aside to give him more room.

"As husband and wife, they must have known we would bathe together," she said taking a small chunk of cheese and pressing the tidbit to his mouth. He took her offering even going so far as to take hold of her hand and suck on the ends of her fingertips. He felt her tremble whilst his lips let go and she then took advantage of the moment to trace his mouth.

By Saint Michael's wings... she was so beautiful and clearly she had no idea what she was doing to him. He would be lucky if he did not release himself before they even made it to the bed.

"I will have to give them a few extra coins to thank them for thinking of such a luxury," Reynard said as he also took up a piece of cheese between his finger and thumb and offered the tasty morsel to the lady.

Her eyes sparkled in delight and she proceeded to copy his actions from but a moment ago. They continued to eat their meal in silence and Reynard began to wonder if she had changed her mind. But while she did not advance their congress, nor did she withdraw. The intimacy of the tub tempted him to take her here and now. Their bodies were already so close she might as well have been on his lap as their legs had become intertwined at their close proximity. He had already been uncomfortable with her riding in his lap for hours. There was only so much one man could take.

Or so he thought... apparently he was in store for so much more when she took the bar of soap and a linen cloth and began to clean her skin. His eyes glazed with need as he was able to watch her curvaceous body or at least what he was allowed to witness above the waterline. But he knew what awaited him soon for he had already seen for himself those perky full breasts, her smooth creamy white skin, and her legs that would wrap around his body perfectly once they were joined as one.

Once she was clean, she tossed him a wicked smile and bent forward. His hungry eyes peered at her in the light of the hearth whilst her own seemed to be glazed in need. She reached out and ran the soapy cloth over his shoulders and arms, over the top of his chest. But she hesitated when she took a glance downward. His eyes silently urged her on and every muscle in his body tensed in anticipation of her touch. He thought he could handle it but he was so wrong.

The moment her delicate hands wrapped around his manhood, he was forced to strain to hold himself in check. How could such an innocent exploration become his undoing? But the pleasure was overwhelming as she ran her fingertips up and down his shaft until he could stand her tender, tentative ministration no further. He took hold of her hand even though such an action about killed him.

"If you do not stop, I will unman myself here and now, my lady," he explained through clenched teeth.

"Does it hurt?" she said appearing worried that she was causing him some sort of injury.

"Hurt?" he said in a strained tone. "God's blood, nay."

"Hmmm," she murmured before she tilted her head to gaze upon him. "I do not wish you to be in pain, Reynard."

"Far from it."

She raised herself on her knees before coming to some decision. The next thing he knew he had his hands full of the woman as she settled herself directly in his lap. The fit was tight given the confines of the tub but she managed to sit there as though she had done this a hundred times.

She bent forward and kissed his lips. "Make me yours in every way, Reynard. Here. Now."

He would not question her demands. He took hold of her

bottom to raise her up until his manhood was at the entrance to her core. "I am sorry this will hurt," he said before plunging past the barrier that proved her innocence.

She cried out, wrapping her arms around his neck, and he waited to move until he could see from her expression that the pain had subsided and she had grown accustomed to his size. She at last took hold of his face and began to kiss him, stealing his breath away as only Elysande could.

Reynard became lost in their play as they began to move in unison in a rhythm known to lovers throughout the ages. But he soon felt the restrictions of their bath and halted their lovemaking. She tossed him a frown before he told her to stand. He followed her as they exited the tub. Before she could lift a foot over the rim, he lifted her up in his arms, carrying her to their bed and not caring that water dripped from their wet bodies. He laid her on top of the coverlets and gazed upon her perfections.

Aye... she was perfect in every way in his mind's eye and he devoured the sight of every inch of her exposed silky skin. She held out her arms to him and he settled himself once more between her legs, taking her own and wrapping them around his waist. Together they moved as though they had been made for one another. Two souls that became one the higher they flew toward the heavens. And when Elysande reached her release calling out his name, he shattered alongside her filling her with his seed. Their breaths were ragged until they both slowed to normal. He rolled over not wanting to crush her with his weight and she settled into his side. Her head lay on his chest and she ran her fingertips over the muscles of his stomach.

He kissed the top of her head. "Next time, we shall start in the bed and 'twill be a perfect coupling."

She gave a contented sigh. "I do not know how our lovemaking could be any more perfect that what we just did."

"We have a lifetime together to find out," he said whilst she continued her play.

"We could find out now," she declared playfully. She raised

her head to gaze upon him whilst her hand reached lower.

"You tempt me but this is new to you and I do not wish you to be in any more pain than I already caused you this eve," he murmured, taking hold of her hand that continued to reach toward his manhood.

"Let me be the judge of that," she said with a laugh. "I am most certain there is more to learn with this lovemaking business and you are just the man to teach me."

A growl left him as he quickly turned so she was once more beneath him. "I am the *only* man who will teach you."

"Then teach me, my love."

He could not refuse such a tempting offer. "As my lady commands…"

Reynard resumed his exploration of his lovely lady and undertook to teach her what he enjoyed far into the night. With the breaking of the dawn, they would both be sleepy eyed but quite well satisfied when they began to ride the remainder of the way to Oxford.

CHAPTER TWENTY-NINE

ELYSANDE AND REYNARD stood before their empress in her solar. The only other people in the room were Richard and his sister Beatrix. It worried Elysande. How severe would the set down be for the empress to feel it should not have an audience? Elysande hung her head whilst the empress bellowed her outrage.

"You ruined her, Norwood. I expected better from you," the empress bellowed.

"She is to be my wife," Reynard declared only to snap his lips shut when the empress pounded on the table next to her with her fist.

"The outcome was for *me* to decide, not for you," she yelled in displeasure.

"You, yourself, declared that the man who rescued Lady Elysande would be allowed to wed her. I was the first to come to her aid. I then announced her publicly to be my wife for her protection when the late hour required us to take shelter in an inn, given that we were unable to reach the castle before the gates closed," Reynard answered, standing tall.

The empress pursed her lips and then inspected Elysande. "Did he take you against your will?"

Elysande jerked her head upright. "Nay!" she proclaimed, taking hold of Reynard's hand. "I willingly gave my consent."

"I will have to take your word for it. You leave me with no other choice than to see that you are properly wed by my priest."

Elysande's smile went wide. "Thank you, my Empress," she

beamed. "I love him very much."

The empress's brow rose. "Love? Bah! A useless emotion. Better to have an arranged marriage for land and titles than for love. But I digress from the point I was attempting to make. I will not have it bandied about my court that one of my ladies in waiting is nothing more than a common whore."

Elysande flinched at the curtness of the words flung about her from the empress. At least there were not many to witness her shame at being called a fallen woman. She should have expected such a reaction from the empress but that did not mean her words did not sting.

There was a sound at the door and the empress called out for whoever was on the other side to enter. Lord Constantine came forward, bowing low.

"Ah, Warin," the empress said waving him to rise. "I suppose you are aware that these… two shall be wed this day."

"I assumed as much, Empress," Constantine declared whilst turning his head to gaze at Elysande and Reynard. "There were no further altercations on your return journey?"

A snort left the empress but she remained silent.

Reynard shook his head. "Nay. There was nothing further to worry over. Did you capture Morcant?"

"'Tis the reason I am here. He is below residing in a cell in our empress's dungeon until she deigns to determine his punishment."

"He is the one who took Lady Elysande?" Beatrix spoke up taking a step forward.

"Aye," Reynard and Constantine answered in unison.

Beatrix gave a heavy sigh. "He always appeared so… nice."

A sound much like a growl left Richard. "You say that about all the men you flirt with. 'Twill be your downfall, sister."

The empress held up her hand. "Silence! Lady Beatrix is not the topic of discussion… at least today. Morcant will be dealt with but first, we have a wedding to see to. Lady Elysande, you and Lady Beatrix may leave so that you may prepare yourself. Meet us in my chapel in an hour. Norwood and Warin... you may remain here and inform me all you learned during your search for Elysande."

Elysande squeezed Reynard's hand, offering him a brief smile before she bowed once again to their empress and left the room with Beatrix. She had her wedding to prepare for and in an hour she would be declared Reynard's wife.

REYNARD LISTENED INTENTLY to Constantine's account of capturing Morcant. The empress had a frown upon her brow to prove she was angry at the details as they unfolded.

Constantine nodded toward Reynard. "You were right about Morcant. He was still sitting in the tavern eating and drinking his fill. He proclaimed his innocence on the matter of taking Elysande right before he yelled at his men to take us out."

"The bloody whoreson," Reynard cursed softly. He mumbled his apology to the empress who gave a wave of her hand for Constantine to continue.

"The altercation inside the confines of a small room were as you might expect. Confusing with tables and chairs being damaged. I paid the owner of the inn for the cost of repairs," Constantine said as though the monies mattered little to him.

"My friends were not injured?" Reynard asked.

"Only mildly. Blake suffered a broken nose but I am certain the ladies will only think he is more appealing once it has healed. Other than that, there were no significant injuries," Constantine replied before he continued. "While Morcant's men were being subdued, he made an attempt to flee out the back door during all the havoc of the fight. Kingsley brought the cur to his knees and tied him up to be transported back to Oxford with his men."

The empress reached for a chalice and took a sip. "It appears you all should be rewarded for your part in capturing the cur," she proclaimed, setting her cup back down, "although I suppose Norwood has the biggest prize of them all."

"A lucky man," Constantine drawled.

The empress gave part of a laugh. "You do not appear very disappointed, Warin. I thought you wished the lady for your wife?"

"I did," he said with a look to Reynard, "but the lady did favor Norwood and I would not truly wish to take a wife who pined away for another."

"Some marriages are made with less," the empress stated.

"Aye, but I should not choose to spend my life with a woman who would never come to care for me. Most unpleasant." Constantine reached out for Reynard and the two men clasped forearms. "I wish you a happy marriage with the lovely Lady Elysande."

Reynard was surprised at the good wishes coming from the man who was once his rival. "My thanks, Warin. May you find your own fair lady soon."

The empress rose. "If the two of you are done making friends with one another, we have a wedding to attend."

Reynard bowed. "What about Morcant?"

"He will be dealt with later once I determine exactly what his punishment will be. In the meantime, he can rot in my dungeon and be thankful he is not residing in the pit."

Reynard went to the door and opened it for the empress, who left them. He inspected what he was wearing and realized he best change and quickly. He would hate to be late for his own wedding.

CHAPTER THIRTY

ELYSANDE INSPECTED HER blue gown one last time. Beatrix adjusted the flowers she had woven into a crown that sat upon Elysande's head. A necklace of blue gems with diamonds had been placed around her neck with the largest of them all nestled just above the cleavage of her breasts. A gift from the empress, or so she had been told by Lady Eden.

Petula stepped forward, placing a kiss on Elysande's cheek. "You are so lucky to be marrying a man you actually love."

Lady Eden agreed. "'Tis a luxury we can only wish to find. We will probably not be as blessed. I am certain that I, at the very least, will one day have an arranged marriage."

Beatrix huffed. "The fact that the empress would allow a tourney to find a husband for one of her ladies does not bode well for the rest of us. At least Reynard was the winner at the end of all the havoc."

Rovena took Elysande's hand. "You look lovely. Be happy."

Elysande could only give a weak smile. Inside, she was quaking in fear that something might happen to cause Reynard to change his mind.

Beatrix took Elysande's hand. "Stop worrying over nothing, Elysande. I know for a fact that Reynard is inside and has not deserted you. If he had, no doubt Richard would have dragged him back by his ear."

A half laugh, half snort escaped her at the vision and she quickly covered her mouth. But there was no mistaking her moment of merriment and the women around Elysande joined in her laughter.

Lady Eden clapped her hands together. "A smiling bride! So much better than what you had plastered on your visage a moment ago. Be happy, Elysande. You are about to be joined in marriage to the man of your dreams."

Petula gave a heavy sigh at such a thought and Elysande could only nod as the women left her, leaving only Beatrix.

"You are lucky to have one of the Norwood brothers love you. I have never met more loyal men than them, mayhap with the exception of my brother. Reynard will never let you down. You can trust him with your heart," Beatrix said squeezing Elysande's hand.

"I never thought I would find someone that I could love like I love Reynard," Elysande whispered, squaring back her shoulders. "I thought I was destined to wander the halls of Blackmore alone for the rest of my days."

Beatrix put her hand on the handle leading to the interior of the chapel. "I cannot imagine such an existence for you or any of the empress's ladies in waiting. I hope love will find me but I will adapt to whatever my fate has in store for me. Now, put a smile back on your face and let us get you wed before Reynard starts yelling to ask what is taking you so long."

Elysande agreed and entered the chapel. The empress sat in the front row with her ladies seated next to her. Reynard stood by the altar with the priest looking splendid in a blue tunic with dark hose. A ceremonial knife was tucked into an embroidered belt at his waist and a chain holding a cross with a dark blue gem hung from his neck. She sighed at the sight of him and could barely contain her joy knowing he was waiting for her.

Her eyes traveled to Hawke sitting next to the rest of Reynard's friends. He nodded his head as she walked past him and Elysande returned her attention to the future that waited for her. Hawke would always be loyal to her but Reynard would now become the center of all she held dear. She stepped forward and gave the man she loved a bright smile.

Reynard took her hands into his warm palms and raised them to kiss the tips of her fingers. "You are beautiful," he murmured whilst those mesmerizing grey eyes held the promise of forever in their depths.

"And you are most handsome, Reynard," she declared, smoothing the fabric at his shoulders once he released her hands.

They turned as one and sat in the front row opposite the empress with Richard, Beatrix and the remaining knights who had come to her rescue directly behind them. Lord Constantine was noticeably absent.

The priest began to drone on about the weakness of the flesh and Elysande peeked at Reynard who was doing his best to hide a smirk. She turned her attention to what the priest was saying. She could not help, however, the memories of their night together that flashed through her mind. At least she knew what their coupling as a married couple this eve would entail. She blushed thinking on the matter and knowing she should be listening to the priest's sermon.

Reynard leaned over to whisper in her ear. "Are you also thinking about tonight, my dear?" he asked in a low sensual tone that caused her body to tingle in delight.

"At least I know what to expect."

"You were more than I *ever* expected to drop into my life."

She tore her gaze from the priest to look upon Reynard. "Complaining already, my love?"

A chuckle rumbled in his chest. "I best not. No sense starting our marriage with a fight."

She smiled knowing he but jested with her. "Smart man."

The priest cleared his throat demanding they return their attention to the matter at hand: his sermon. Elysande could barely sit there quietly when all she wished for was the lecture to be over so they could speak the words that would seal them together. The priest at last finished and called for the scribe who rushed forward with quill and parchment. He went to a small table set up for his use and nodded to the priest who then asked for an accounting of what each brought to their union.

Richard stepped forward offering a sum large enough to have Reynard choke in surprise at his friend's generosity. Blake, Oswin, and Kingsley repeated the gesture and Elysande swore there was a moment where she could see Reynard's eyes glisten with an unshed tear or two. The priest then turned toward Elysande. But there was no one to speak on her behalf so she rose from her place next to Reynard.

"Blackmore Castle was granted to me upon my grandfather's death and comes with forty acres of surrounding land," Elysande began with a worried frown. Blackmore was in need of major repairs. It might take years to see the estate returned to what it had once been. She glanced at Reynard, knowing what a burden her home would become to her new husband. The monies needed to restore Blackmore would be excessive, and she did not wish to ask Reynard to sacrifice any of his wealth to see her home restored. 'Twas a lot to ask.

She bit her lip, knowing she did not have much else to offer for the scribe. Her parents had land abroad in Normandy and more in England. Those estates, as far as Elysande knew, were full of cattle, horses, and other animals but since she had never been there, she was unfamiliar with the management of said estates nor could she claim ownership of them whilst her parents yet lived.

The empress stood. "Lady Elysande was promised a substantial dowry once my games were concluded. I stand by my decision. Ample monies will fill her and her new husband's coffers," Matilda exclaimed with a smile before she continued, "enough to see Blackmore restored to all its former glory so that the Lord and Lady of Blackmore might continue their pledged fealty to me."

"Thank you, empress," Elysande answered, dropping down into a deep curtsey. Reynard took to his knee and bowed his head before they were both told to rise.

Overall, the empress had just made Elysande quite rich.

But 'twas the slight frown on Reynard's brow that caused her to worry. "You appear upset," Elysande said watching him carefully.

"You have become a very wealthy woman," he declared, gulping.

"You are also a rich man."

A grunt escaped him. "Only from the generosity of friends."

She smiled. "I was not necessarily thinking of the monies they gave you. Sometimes there is more to life than the monies that fill your coffers. Those men love you like brothers. Surely that in itself is worth more than anything else."

He ran his thumb over the back of her hand. "Aye… I suppose you are right."

The priest asked them to step forward and before long he was proclaiming them husband and wife. Reynard quickly kissed her lips, and the empress clapped her hands, causing everyone's attention to turn.

"Well done," she proclaimed, then took the place of the priest. "Take a knee, Norwood."

Elysande gasped at the significance of what she asked and Reynard's eyes widened in surprise. He did as he was told and Empress Matilda held out her hand. Lady Eden brought forward a ceremonial blade. The empress then tapped the blade on Reynard's right shoulder and repeated the gesture on his left.

"Rise, Reynard Norwood, Earl of Blackmore," the empress proclaimed. A small cheer rose up.

Elysande threw her arms around her husband's neck once he stood and proceeded to kiss him. He snaked his arm around her waist and pulled her up against his rock-hard chest and deepened their kiss. Not only had they been married but Reynard had been more than rewarded for his service to the empress's cause. Their life together was off to a wonderful start.

CHAPTER THIRTY-ONE

REYNARD WATCHED HIS wife as she performed the patterns of a dance with Richard. Her laughter rang out and he wished he had been the one to cause her such joy. Wife… if someone had told him a year ago that he would be wed at the age of a score and three he would have laughed in their face. The twist and turns that life had thrown in the path of the Norwood brothers had changed their lives for the better. All three wed to beautiful women who were more than worthy of them. Reynard was still in a daze from all that had occurred just this day.

Married and then a short moment later a titled lord. Who would have known that the generosity of Empress Matilda would have gone that far? Reynard had expected such of Wymar for he was the head of the family. But Theobald and he had also gained far more than Reynard ever thought possible. His eyes searched for his wife who had disappeared amongst the dancers. Not that he was worried. Richard was like his brother and Reynard knew Elysande was as safe with Richard as if she stood next to him now. Perchance love would also find Grancourt soon.

A voice from behind him brought Reynard out of his musings.

"Have you lost your bride so soon, Norwood?"

Reynard barely acknowledged Constantine as he came to stand beside him. "Nay, I have not," he said reaching for a tankard of ale from a passing servant. "I did not see you at the wedding."

A grunt of displeasure escaped Constantine's mouth. "There is only so much suffering one man can stand. I had come to admire the lady, not that I would voice such feelings aloud when she clearly cared for another."

"You did not protest at all that Elysande and I were to wed," Reynard replied, watching Constantine closely. Could he have been mistaken thinking Warin had moved past his feelings for Elysande?

Constantine shrugged as though indifferent. "I had no objections to you wedding the lady but that does not mean I needed to bear witness to the ceremony. We would have still made a good matched if the empress had blessed our union."

"For an arranged marriage," grumbled Reynard, taking another long pull of his drink.

"Some have married for far less," Constantine suggested. "I am surprised you have not whisked your beautiful bride to your chambers. I assure you, if she were mine, we would already be upstairs." A chuckle rumbled in his chest when he looked over to Reynard who could only scowl at his rival.

"'Tis none of your business when I take my wife to our bedchamber," Reynard finally replied as the music shifted as the song came to an end and another began. Hawke took his turn to dance with Elysande and Reynard could hear her laughter from where he stood.

Constantine threw up his hand and laughed. "Far be it from me to advise you on how to run your marriage. I will bow down to the better man who captured her… heart."

Reynard was about to reply when Constantine raised his own cup in a salute and walked away. Reynard watched him leave. The man was quickly surrounded by several women of the court. He would not lack for companionship this eve if he so chose.

Enough of Warin, he thought. He had better things in mind than a man who one moment was helping him locate Elysande and the next appeared almost jealous. Elysande waved from across the great hall when her dance with Hawke was finished and Reynard began making his way through the crowded room to reach her side. She wound her arms around his neck and he pulled her close whilst inhaling the smell of roses that came from her hair.

"Are you enjoying our wedding celebration, my dear?" Reynard murmured whilst a part of him began to rise given their close proximity. God's blood... what this woman did to him with the briefest touch!

"I am, but I have not seen you amongst the dancers," she replied. She began twirling a length of his dark brown hair and 'twas hard to keep his hands to himself.

"I would rather watch you dance than join in with a woman who is anyone but... you."

"I did not realize I had married someone so romantic," she teased, and her eyes appeared to sparkle in the torchlight of the room.

"Only for you..." His reply hopefully had an underlying tone that suggested they head upstairs, but he did not want to take away her happiness if she wished to continue the celebration happening in the great hall.

Her smile was so sweet and innocent that he wanted to run his fingers through her hair and enjoy the remainder of the eve in the privacy of their chamber. He bent down to capture her lips and she molded her body close to his own. 'Twas all the encouragement he needed, and he crushed her into his embrace. Her breath hitched, and Reynard knew without any doubt she could tell how ready he was to make her his in every way.

"Perchance no one would miss us if we were to continue our celebration privately?" she suggested with a seductive smile that reminded him of seeing her naked and about to step in that tub at the inn.

"I suspect they wonder why we have not left hours ago," he said with a grin.

"You rogue," she teased, running her hand up and down the front of his tunic. "I suppose we should ask the empress for permission to leave?"

He briefly took his eyes from his wife to see that the empress was deep in conversation. "She will not miss us. If you are ready, let us go upstairs."

She nodded and took his hand. They stayed composed by slowly walking and nodding to the other lords and ladies as they headed toward the turret. But once out of view, they began to run up the stairs, down the passageway, and threw the bolt as soon as they gained access to the bedchamber.

"Good eve to you, wife," Reynard said in a husky whisper. He untied the belt at his waist, letting it drop to the floor, and then pulled his tunic over his head. His eyes roamed over every inch of the woman who had stolen his heart with just one look.

"Glad tidings to you, husband," she answered, looking over her shoulder. She pulled the wreath from her head, carefully placing the flowers on the table before she opened her arms to him. He wasted no time shortening the distance between them and he lifted her with one arm. He swung her around, and her head tilted back in delight.

"You are happy." His words were more of a declaration than a question.

"So happy that I must be dreaming," Elysande replied as her body skimmed down his chest.

"Then we are sharing the same dream. I could not be happier than to have you as my bride."

"I swear I became lost the moment I gazed into your grey eyes," she said contently. "Well... mayhap not at first glance but there was still something there."

He gave a light chuckle. "And I was found the moment I looked into your blue ones."

She took her fingers and brushed them over his cheek. "I love you."

He took both her cheeks in his calloused hands. "As I love you, Elysande. For today, tomorrow and for always."

"Then kiss me and make me yours... again," she purred, and

he wasted no time pulling her gown away from her body. Her jewels came next along with her under clothing, and a pile of linen began to form on the floor. She jumped onto the bed, and he went to sit on the edge to remove his boots. She molded herself to his back and his breath caught in his throat at the feel of her warm skin next to his own.

"Hurry..." she urged and he did as she commanded for he could barely hold himself back from taking her there and now.

But he had other plans, and he took his time exploring every inch of the body that was exposed beneath his gaze. When he could finally stand their play no longer, he knew she was more than ready for him when he heard a moan of pleasure escape her lips. And just when he thought he could not hold off any longer, they shattered together as they each yelled out the other's name. They had climbed to the heavens and seen the stars together, forever becoming one with their release. Surely God above had blessed their union, and Reynard would give further praise to Him come the morning Mass that He had put Elysande in his path.

He was, indeed, a lucky man.

CHAPTER THIRTY-TWO

September 1142

ELYSANDE'S DAYS CONTINUED to be busy. She still attended the empress although her duties had lessened somewhat now that she was a married woman. But her nights… Her nights were filled with bliss laying in Reynard's arms. Her husband had a voracious appetite as he taught her all the things he enjoyed in their marriage bed. She was more than a willing participant and she soon learned a trick or two of her own to ensure they were both satisfied. In many ways, she could never get enough of her husband and this, too, seemed to please him immensely. Some morns, they did not wish to leave their bed.

Lord Constantine returned to his home without a bride and in a way, Elysande was sad to see him go. He had become a friend. If someone had told her such might happen when they first met she would have sworn they jested with her. But he was content to have seen her happily married, or so he had informed her when he departed.

Gerold Morcant was not as lucky. After a brief audience with Empress Matilda, he and the knight who had taken her from her bedchamber were returned to their cells in Oxford's dungeon. They would remain there as a constant reminder of how close the empress might have been to her own abduction. Elysande was only too happy to see him dragged away in chains.

Another gift from the empress came when she told Elysande she would be sending masons to work on the walls in need of repair back at Blackmore. She had also said she would ensure the outbuildings would be repaired, the livestock restocked, and serfs and servants sent to work the land and castle. Come the winter, the majority of the work that needed to be done should be in place except for the curtain and battlement walls. Those could take years to complete but 'twas a start. Elysande was looking for the day they would be released from their service to the empress and she and Reynard could return there to live, but aside from a wish for home, she could not be happier.

But not everything was perfect—at least in the outside world. Elysande was privy to conversations between the empress and her advisers that Elysande never thought she would ever hear. Clearly, Elysande had earned the woman's trust and confidence to be entrusted with such sensitive information. The court moved from one location to the next, and Elysande and Reynard moved with her to her castle in Devizes in order for her to meet with her half-brother Robert and her other advisors. Reynard was ever vigilant in protecting not only his wife but his empress.

The envoys who had been sent to Normandy with a message to Empress Matilda's husband, Geoffrey, back in April finally returned in June. They did not bear good news as her husband refused to negotiate terms with anyone other than Earl Robert. With other news that King Stephen had fallen ill the previous month, the empress thought she would remain safe if she returned to Oxford since the stronghold was a stone fortress. The earl protested but eventually conceded to his sister's request, and he rode for Wareham in Dorset. The port was still under the empress's control and in the hands of Robert's eldest son, William. He then took a ship for Normandy.

Meanwhile, the empress and her people returned to Oxford Castle with the thought that she would be closer to London to claim the throne when Stephen died. News of his recovery hit the empress hard, and Elysande pondered to herself if the empress would ever sit on England's throne. It was beginning to seem unlikely.

A pounding of someone's fist on the table tore Elysande out of her musings. The scowl on Richard Grancourt's face more than told the mood of those in the room. "Stephen and his men have taken Wareham and the castle there," he snarled as he tossed the missive he had been reading onto the table.

The empress all but folded herself into a chair. "That will leave my brother without a port to land in once he finally returns to England."

Reynard picked up the parchment and scanned it before he passed it to the next knight standing beside him. "Stephen will not stop with capturing Wareham, especially if he is aware that the empress is without her brother, who has been her main supporter."

"I was a fool to send Robert abroad but what else could I do? I thought I would be safe without him," the empress said clearly worried about the coming months.

"You *are* safe here, Empress," Richard said, trying to reassure her. "We will not allow anyone to take you."

There were several *here, here*'s called out by the men present.

The empress nodded to her loyal knights. "You have been protecting me faithfully for some time now. I do not expect you to fail me anytime soon."

Reynard stepped forward. "We are your most humble servants," he declared. But when his gazed traveled to Elysande, she could tell that her husband was worried.

The conversations turned to preparing for the worst while hoping that nothing would come from their enemy. But based on her own past experience with Stephen's men, even Elysande could see that there was cause for concern. When the men began to disperse, Reynard asked to speak to his wife. The empress consented, and they went to their chamber. Reynard began to pace.

"Should I be worried?" Elysande asked in concern.

He watched her carefully and she went to stand near the window. She turned away to open the wooden shutter, hoping that a breath of fresh air might calm her nerves. It did not have the outcome she had hoped for even as she took several deep breaths. Reynard came and pulled her back into his chest whilst he leaned his chin on the top of her head.

"Aye," he finally muttered. "I wish we were far away from Oxford, but I cannot in good faith leave the empress now. Not when her life might be in danger in the coming months. Mayhap we should arrange for you to travel to Blackmore. You would be far safer at home than you are here."

"Nay," she sobbed. "I will not leave you and you cannot make me."

Reynard turned her to face him and ran a finger down her cheek. "I would rather have you safe at Blackmore than watch you starve if this castle comes under a siege."

Elysande put her arms around his waist. "'Twould not be the first time I went to bed with an empty stomach. Or did you already forget the fine meal I prepared for you the day you showed up at my castle?"

"Your attempt to put humor into this conversation is failing, my lady. How do you expect me to watch the woman I love go hungry?" he demanded.

She arched one of her dark brows. "And you think 'twill be any easier on me to watch my husband grow weak from lack of food?" she asked.

"You need not watch. I can easily have several trusted knights escort you home."

"I know you can, but I am not leaving. Not without you."

He threw up his hands in frustration and tried again. "Please go home to Blackmore, Elysande. 'Twould ease my conscience if I have one less thing to worry over."

"I can take care of myself," she declared in a firm tone.

"I have never met such a stubborn lady. Why will you not obey my commands?"

"If you wanted a woman to obey your every whim and always allow you to order her about, then you should have married another woman."

A heavy sigh escaped him. "I only wish to keep you safe… at Blackmore."

"Blackmore is no safer than any other place in England whilst Stephen holds the throne. I wish I could obey your suggestion but as I just said… not without you," Elysande replied, taking a seat by the hearth.

"You are a tenacious woman, Elysande Norwood," he muttered, coming to kneel down before her.

"You knew that before we wed. You had your chance to escape, but you chose to persist, so you are now stuck with me," she said and began to brush a lock of his dark brown hair back into place that had fallen over his forehead.

Reynard took her hand, pressing his lips to the inside of her wrist. His grey eyes met hers. "What am I to do with you?"

She gave him a smile that she hoped reached into his soul. "Why such a question is easy to answer, my love."

He gave her a roguish smirk as if he could read her thoughts. "And what is your reply, lovely Elysande?"

She leaned forward to place her lips upon his and then gave him his answer. "Just love me…"

CHAPTER THIRTY-THREE

REYNARD SWUNG HIS blade in a wide arc, but he failed to hit his target. He ducked, narrowly missing the sword aimed at his head. Uttering a curse, he pushed forward to slay the knight who had attempted to slice his head from his neck. The knight was briefly distracted, lowering his guard, and Reynard found his opportunity delivering the fatal blow. He witnessed the man's eyes go wide in disbelief behind his iron helm before he fell backward. Placing his boot on the dead man's chest, Reynard yanked hard to pull his sword free. He barely had time to wipe the steel on the tunic of his fallen enemy before another foe took his place.

There was always another adversary attempting to take the life of himself and those who fought for the empress, at least of late. Stephen had quickly recuperated from whatever ailment had overtaken him, and with his recovery he went on the attack. But he did not initially attack Oxford where he knew Empress Matilda was staying. Nay… instead he burned, looted, and overtook surrounding castles and land, cutting off any supplies or necessities that might have seen to the survival of those within the city of Oxford and its keep.

Based on the council Reynard had been privy to, the empress thought Oxford would remain a safe haven. After all, the city was surrounded by a deep river. But she was still outnumbered and without additional troops from her brother Robert, there were not any to call upon for reinforcement. Not when every castle close to Oxford had also seen its fair share of war.

When word had reached them that Stephen's troops were on the outskirts of the city, the empress went mad with rage. Calling up her men, she had them raise their swords outside the city gates, but by now Reynard could see that their forces were dwindling. They needed to retreat to the main gate of the keep before all was lost.

He swung his sword again in an automatic movement to stay alive. Oswin and Blake were nearby to his left, holding their own. Kingsley was to his right, and if he did not turn in time, he would find himself stabbed in the back.

"Goodee," Reynard bellowed above the noise of the battle. "Behind you!"

Kingsley rapidly whirled around, raising his arm in time to block the blade aimed at his back. He began to fiercely hack away at his enemy until he was able to send his opponent stumbling over another dead body. As he staggered, Kingsley pushed his blade forward, ending the man's life. When he did not immediately see another foe who would attempt to slay him, he searched the area and finally espied Reynard. Kingsley gave him a jaunty salute in thanks for Reynard's warning before once again going on the attack.

That left the whereabouts of Richard unknown. Reynard had little time to randomly look around for the man, but Wymar would skewer Reynard alive if he allowed anything to happen to Richard if 'twas in Reynard's power to prevent such an outcome. Family meant everything to the Norwood brothers, and Richard had long been considered a part of it. But war was a messy business, especially when there was barely had time to breathe whilst defeating one enemy after another.

He finally caught a glimpse of Grancourt who was battling against a knight much smaller than him. Why, the knight could not be much more than a lad who had just earned his spurs, based on his height. 'Twas almost unfair that Richard continued his assault on such a young knight but surprisingly, he held his own against the seasoned warrior.

Knowing there was not much time left for him and the others to reach the keep with Stephen's army continuing to surge forward to seize the day, Reynard began hacking his way toward Richard to catch his attention.

"Richard!" Reynard bellowed over the noise of clashing swords. "We must flee to the keep."

"Not without taking this one with us," Richard yelled back over his shoulder.

"Leave him," Reynard yelled before smashing his fist into the face of the knight before him.

"I cannot," Richard exclaimed as he took on another knight who came to assist the younger one.

Reynard cursed, swinging his blade again to fell another enemy. "He may be small, but he shall survive the onslaught of this skirmish. Besides… he is a traitor by swearing his allegiance to the usurper."

"You do not understand, Reynard," Richard said as he took another life and turned his attention back to the young boy who now held his blade in front of him with both hands, his strength clearly waning.

"What is there to understand?"

Richard lowered his blade momentarily before he answered. The young knight took a swipe at Richard and missed whilst Richard leapt forward, capturing the boy around the waist. He brought the squirming lad up to his chest and yanked the helmet from his head.

"She's a woman!" Richard finally answered when he revealed a long tawny colored braid that had been hiding beneath her chainmail. Green eyes flashed angrily at Reynard when he drew near.

"Bloody hell… another one," Reynard cursed. "Why are these women always showing up on a battlefield where they do not belong?"

The woman continued to struggle against Richard's grip on

her. "Get your bloody hands of me," she swore, stomping her boot on Richard's foot.

"Hold still, you little hellion," Richard said whilst holding her tighter.

"You have no right to take me prisoner," the woman hissed, fruitlessly trying to break free as Richard towered over her.

"You and I have met before briefly at Winchester," Richard said as he began tugging her along toward the keep. "I lost you once before and have no intention of doing so again so you can wreak further mayhem on the empress's army."

"You know nothing about me and have no right," she called out again.

Reynard smirked. "You have your hands full with this one, Richard, but you best hasten. Decide immediately if you plan to take her with us or else let the lady go. 'Tis no time to dally with a woman when we must needs still fight our way to the keep. I'd advise leaving her. She will only hinder you."

No sooner had Reynard's words left his mouth, then Stephen's forces pressed forward. Richard lost his grip on the woman knight, and he watched her flee from sight.

"Damn it," Richard cursed, but he had no chance to run after her when he had his hands full fighting to stay alive.

A trumpet sounded in the distance and Reynard and Richard shared a knowing look between them. They fought their way toward the gate leading to the castle, avoiding one blade after another to stay alive. They barely made it before the barbican gate shut into place, its deadly porticus burying itself deep into the ground.

Their breathing ragged, Reynard hunched over, putting his hands on his legs and taking deep, long breaths to calm himself. Knights began turning a large wheel whilst another door was slowly lowered into place for protection of those on the other side. 'Twould not take long before machines of war were built to destroy the barriers that were currently keeping them safe... at least for a while.

Richard and Reynard clasped hands and were soon met with Blake, Oswin, and Kingsley. They were all still alive to fight another day, but Reynard had a feeling in his gut that 'twould be months before they all might taste freedom again. Oxford Castle was now under a heavy siege and he, Elysande, his friends, and even Empress Matilda were going nowhere.

CHAPTER THIRTY-FOUR

ELYSANDE STOOD ATOP the battlement wall of the keep. Her knuckles were white from her tight grip on the stone barrier. Black plumes billowed from the many fires that burned through-out the city of Oxford, turning the sky dark. The taste of ash and smoke had formed on her lips causing her to choke. Somewhere down below, Empress Matilda's knights continued to fight in her name hoping to prevent Stephen's army from gaining access into the interior of the city. But their quest had failed. Now Elysande could only pray that her husband was still alive somewhere down below among the havoc of those making their way to the castle for protection.

The empress stood next to Elysande with Lady Eden on the opposite side. Beatrix, Petula and Rovena stood behind as though afraid to get near the edge of the wall.

"We are doomed," Petula whined and then proceeded to break down in a crying fit.

The empress looked at the two ladies standing behind her. "Take her below, Lady Rovena. The last thing I need right now is to hear one of my ladies whining about our circumstances."

"As you wish, Empress," Rovena replied, taking Petula's arm and guiding her toward the entrance to the stairs.

Beatrix came to stand next to Elysande and clasped her hand. "I pray Richard has survived."

Elysande briefly stole a glance at the older woman. "I'm sure he has. There is too much fight in him than to let an enemy defeat him."

"You sound so sure," Beatrix said as though she doubted Elysande's words.

"If he is anything like these Norwood brothers I have heard so much about then, aye, I am certain he will survive, much like my own Reynard," Elysande declared with a confident smile.

"I wish I could share your sentiments, Elysande," Beatrix said. Elysande watched her chin quiver in doubt and worry over her sibling.

The empress gave a sound much like a grunt of displeasure. "If you cannot be optimistic that my most loyal knights will survive this skirmish, Lady Beatrix, then you may also go below to cower in fear."

Beatrix held her tongue and lowered her eyes. Her lips began to silently move as if in prayer.

Silence continued from the women who remained by the empress's side as they endured the torment of the scene before them. Clashing swords rang out amongst the sounds of those who battled one another to gain another foot of ground. They came closer by the moment, and inside, Elysande was quaking in fear knowing what was to soon come. The empress's men would not win this fight, not when she did not have Earl Robert and the reinforcements she had hoped he would bring from her husband in Normandy. Nay, a siege was imminent, and Elysande dreaded the moment when the barbican gate would shut out the outside world and doom them to their fate.

The empress looked over her shoulder to a knight standing near the entrance to the stairs. "Sound the alarm for the gates to close," she ordered.

The knight stepped forward and began to blare the ivory olifant signaling a warning to those still without Oxford Castle's gates. The empress's knights began to enter the bailey whilst others went to stand at the ready to close the portcullis and barbican gate at the gatehouse.

The empress took Elysande's hand and repeated the gesture

to Eden. A rare show of affection to two women she trusted. She was as worried as the rest of them but continued to show her bravery even though she surely also trembled in fear.

"They will make it through the gates. I have no doubt," the empress murmured and Elysande felt her hand squeezed.

"Aye. I believe you, Empress," Elysande replied, searching the bailey below for signs of Reynard. Her heart lurched seeing those entering and the wounds that would need to be cared for.

Eden leaned forward to peer below. "Many will be in need of our care to see to their injuries."

The empress nodded. "Go see what you can begin doing for them. Linens torn into strips for binding their wounds, hot water, and whatever else you can think of."

Eden quickly left and the three women continued to watch the chaos below. "They will be hungry, too, I imagine," Elysande said, thinking her thoughts aloud.

"We will need to survey what food supplies we have in the storehouse and cellars below. I imagine we will be without reinforcements for perhaps months and will need to ration out what we have amongst us."

"We will survive this, Empress," Elysande said. She could fill her voice with confidence since she had already survived this once before. How much harder could the situation be this time around? As more men began to pour through the gates, she had her answer. Much harder given the number of mouths that would need to be fed on whatever limited supplies they had on hand.

The empress turned her gaze to Elysande. "You are made of stern stuff, Elysande Norwood. You would have to be since you wed into the Norwood family. I have never met such loyal men, not only to me but to their spouses. You do your husband credit."

Elysande was momentarily shocked by such a confession from the empress. "You are too kind, Empress," Elysande replied once she found her voice.

"We will have to plan a strategy not only to survive but to

retaliate against Stephen whilst we are locked up here in this tower. I suspect he will soon build his machines of war to tear down these walls that for now keep us safe."

"You have nothing to fear, Empress. Your men will keep you well protected," Elysande said confidently.

A weak smile appeared on her face. "I may always show the outside world and the men who follow me that I am strong and in command of all those who serve me, but even I sometimes have a moment where fear creeps into my heart. Not that I would allow such an emotion to overcome me."

Elysande felt the empress squeeze her hand again before she let go. Clearly, her few moments of needing reassurance were over. The empress was once more the stern and commanding woman that Elysande had pledged her fealty to.

The empress pointed down below. "Ah! Here they are at last. Goodee, Woodwarde, Kennarde…" the empress began, "… and lastly Grancourt and Norwood. They made it. Go see to your husband, and I shall start planning my revenge."

Elysande breathed a sigh of relief even as the portcullis shut, and the distant sound of the barbican gate fell into place. They were safe for now—but for how long, no one could predict. In the meantime, she quickly made her way down to find Reynard, all the while praying he did not sustain any injury that might cost him his life.

Once she made it down to the inner bailey, she found it crowded with knights either being attended to or being helped into the great hall where everyone's injuries could be seen and taken care of. Elysande searched for Reynard and finally espied him with his friends whilst they had all gathered in a circle and held onto each other's shoulders. A rare sight: men loyal to not only the empress but one another. They had all survived the battle outside of these gates and Elysande was grateful, but when the men broke apart, she cared for naught but flinging herself into Reynard's arms.

He gave a grunt of surprise telling her that somewhere on his body he was injured. He started to pull her away from his body, but she clung to him as she cried in relief that he yet lived.

"Elysande, you shall ruin your gown," Reynard stated as he kissed the top of her head.

"I do not care about my gown," she muttered in relief that she was once more in his arms.

"I care about your gown and the stench that covers me." He finally managed to pry her arms from around his neck and gazed down upon her. He placed a quick kiss upon her lips. "There are many that need our aid so I will see you later this eve."

"What about you? Where are you hurt?" she pleaded as she roamed her eyes up and down his body. He was covered in blood, and she refused to see what had transferred onto her own gown. Clothes could be laundered. Her husband's well-being was at the forefront of her mind.

"Nothing that cannot be easily stitched later, my love. Now let us see to those who are not as fortunate," he replied, taking her hand and leading her to a group of knights who lay upon the ground moaning.

After that brief encounter, Elysande lost all sense of time as she tended to one fallen knight after the next. 'Twould be some time long into the evening before she herself would be able for find some comfort and rest.

$$\cdot\!\!\!-\!\!\!-\!\!\!\cdot\!\!\!-\!\!\!\cdot\!\!\!-\!\!\!\cdot\!\!\!-\!\!\!-\!\!\!\cdot$$

CHAPTER THIRTY-FIVE

REYNARD LOOKED OVER the map of Oxford Castle and the outlying area. There were not many in the empress's solar for this discussion. Their fate was grim at best. Supplies were running out since Stephen had instituted a blockade, barring the way to any sources that would bring food and other necessities into the castle. The harbor was also blocked from what they could gather and any hope that Robert of Gloucester would arrive to rescue them diminished whilst each day rolled into the next.

'Twas now almost mid-December and they had been held inside these walls since September. And while the empress had sent her calvary out to call upon those who still favored her before the gates closed months ago, no one had been able to come to her aid or bring reinforcements. She was tired, cold, and hungry as were the rest of them but she would no longer stay idly by and starve to death. Instead, she planned her own escape.

The empress pointed to the postern gate that opened outside the city. "This is the best option for my plan to work," she said, looking upon Reynard, Richard, Blake, and Kingsley.

Reynard frowned. "'Tis extremely risky, Empress," he stated the obvious. "We will have to navigate right through the middle of Stephen's troops."

"Aye," Richard proclaimed, "and we will have a river to cross if the ice holds."

"'Twill be the death of us if it does not," Kingsley interjected.

The empress began to pace the floor. "I will not let an icy river deter me from escaping Stephen's clutches nor will I sit here any longer without food and wood for our fires. If we can escape undetected, Stephen will eventually become aware that I am no longer inside Oxford. He will then have no choice but to allow those who remain to surrender."

"'Tis the best plan we have," Reynard said raising his hand to his chin. "If it works, he will be furious."

Richard chuckled. "I would like to see his reaction that he was thwarted again by our empress."

A smirk turned up at the corners of the empress's mouth. "That would be a sight to see—not that we shall be anywhere near the man to witness such a reaction. For this to work, I think 'twill be best if we keep our numbers small. No more than three or four of you should come with me."

The men swore at such a thought and Richard held up his hand to silence them. "Think about it, men. If our numbers are smaller, then 'twill be easier to make our way unseen through Stephen's troops."

"We shall wear white," the empress suggested. "'Twill provide camouflage for us to blend in with the snow."

Blake leaned on the table whilst still viewing the map. "What of your ladies? Surely, the trek across the countryside will be too much for them."

Empress Matilda shook her head. "Aye. You are right. They cannot come with me and will have to remain here. We shall leave Oswin here so he may watch over them to ensure they come to no harm.

'Twas Reynard's turn to shake his head in displeasure. He did not relish leaving Elysande behind. "He will not wish to remain behind. He has been with you as long as the rest of us."

Richard went and poured himself a cup of wine. "You will need at least one of your ladies to be with you. What about my sister?"

"Are you mad, Grancourt? I would go insane having Beatrix

forced upon me. Nay. She stays here," the empress ordered, then turned to Reynard. "Bring Elysande. That woman has endured much. A little foul weather should not hinder her ability to keep up with us on our little adventure."

A snort left Kingsley. "An adventure, Empress?" he muttered. "We will likely be holding our breath from the moment we leave the gate and thrust ourselves at our enemies' feet."

Reynard saw another problem. "'Twould not be easy to leave behind Elysande's captain. Elysande will most likely ask for Hawke de Challon to accompany her. He has been a most trusted guardsman since the time she was a young girl."

The empress tapped a finger on the wooden table. "That's one too many knights, I think," she answered. "'Tis best he also stay behind with Woodwarde to help guard those who remain here. When do you propose we begin this escapade?"

Reynard was already dreading telling Elysande that Hawke would not travel with them. "We should wait until the middle of the night when their camp is quiet and Stephen's men are asleep. Certainly, we can hide ourselves well enough to avoid any guards who are patrolling at such an ungodly hour," Reynard suggested.

The empress gave her approval. "You are my most trusted men and I know you will see me through this. If we can make it across the river Thames, then we can make our way to Abingdon."

Blakes's eyes widened. "That is another six miles, Empress. Will you be able to make it that far on foot?"

The empress threw up her hands. "What choice do I have? I know this will work. Go prepare yourselves. And Norwood... make sure Elysande is ready to leave with us."

Reynard and the men bowed and left the solar. In the passageway, the men gathered around one another.

"I will go tell Oswin he is to stay behind. Mayhap he will not be too disappointed when he learns Beatrix will also be left here," Kingsley said before leaving to go find their friend.

Richard cursed. "Now I will have to worry whether my sister

is behaving the whole time we are gone."

Reynard laughed. "'Twill hardly be the first time you were bothered over what your little sister was plotting inside her head."

Blake joined in. "Aye... you may need to attend another wedding soon if she is not careful." Richard lunged at Blake who held up his hands. "Do not take out your frustration on me. 'Tis best to have a conversation with the lady before she finds we are gone come the morn."

Reynard ran his hand over the back of his neck. "I had best find Elysande if she is to travel with us. Let us hope we can find enough white linen so we will blend in with the environment."

They all bid a hasty farewell with an agreement to meet up at the appointed time. Reynard went to his chamber and found Elysande sitting near the hearth. There was a white cloth on her lap and she was applying a needle and thread to the garment. He should not have been surprised that she was already aware of the situation that would shortly unfold. He shut the door to the bedchamber and slid the bolt into place.

"You know..."

She raised her head whilst her blue eyes scanned his features. A small smile lit her face. "The empress told me her plan this morn after dismissing her other ladies. I assume she convinced you and the rest of your friends into accepting her escape plan."

"'Tis a good plan," Reynard said, crossing the room and placing a kiss upon her lips.

"Except that I will be left behind whilst you go to protect our empress. You might be captured, and I will never know your fate," she proclaimed, heaving a heavy sigh, bowing her head.

He came to kneel before her. "You *will* know because you are going with me."

She raised her head and eyes to search his face. "Truly?"

"Aye, but be aware, the going will not be easy. If you think you are freezing now, that will be nothing compared to sneaking through an enemy camp and then trudging another six miles or more in the snow until we reach safety."

She grabbed his hand. "I can do it."

"I know you can but that does not mean I do not worry. 'Tis enough to make an escape with the empress. 'Tis another situation entirely to be dragging my wife along."

"As long as we are together, I can endure anything."

"You say that now when we are protected against the elements," he grumbled, coming to a stand. He went to a table that held a pitcher of wine and poured himself a cup, thankful that there was even this remaining luxury. He took a sip deep in thought and did not hear Elysande when she came up behind him. She put her arms around his waist and rested her head on his back.

"I will not be a burden to you or the empress, especially since she asked for me to accompany her. I have spent the entire day working on our cloaks," she said squeezing him tight.

He placed the cup down and turned, taking her in his arms. "I do not suppose I can convince you to stay here where I know you will be safe."

Elysande gave him a look that spoke volumes. "We have had this discussion before, my love. How safe can I be with the usurper right outside these very gates?"

"He will leave and accept the surrender of those who remain once he learns the empress is no longer here." He picked up his cup and took another drink.

"You cannot be certain of that. Already his machines of war relentlessly bombard the castle and the surrounding areas. He has blocked off everything and is slowly starving us out," she answered. She waved her finger at the cup he still held. "And you best enjoy that chalice of wine for that is the last of it."

He turned the cup and offered her to take it. "Share it with me." He swore her eyes sparkled mischievously whilst watching him. She licked her lips before placing her mouth where his had been but moments ago. "A lover's gesture…"

"Aye," she whispered handing him the cup that he set down

upon the table. Her fingertips began smoothing down the fabric of his tunic. "Mayhap instead of arguing about whether I stay here or go with you, we can do something else to occupy the time before we are to leave."

"Does my wife have something in mind?" he asked in a husky tone.

Elysande tugged on his hand, leading him to their bed, not that he objected. "I'm sure we can think of something."

He sat on the edge of the bed and pulled her down with him. "I am yours to command, my lady wife."

"Finally… you listen to me," she teased before giving him a quick kiss and wiggling her body over his. He took hold of the back of her neck bringing her closer.

"Mayhap just this once…"

There was no further need for words when she kissed him thoroughly and he proceeded to make love to his lady as though it might be the last time. He did not know what the middle of the night would bring, nor come the morn, but whatever their fate, Reynard and Elysande would meet the challenge together.

CHAPTER THIRTY-SIX

E LYSANDE PULLED THE edges of her cloak closer to her neck as she and the small company gathered around their empress whilst making their way to the postern gate. 'Twas the first time that she could remember where Hawke did not accompany her and she already felt the loss of his presence. Elysande had no notion as to the time of night other than 'twas late and no man or beast should be braving the bitter cold of this winter's eve. But the brisk chill in the air and the snow that blanketed the earth fit in perfectly with the empress's plans to make her escape.

Richard turned to address the group before opening the gate door. "Remember… your silence is imperative to this plan working. We must needs tread carefully once outside this gate as our enemy will be near at every turn."

The empress took hold of Richard's arm. "Let us proceed, Grancourt. We have a long journey ahead of us once we cross the river."

Elysande gulped, thinking of the mighty Thames River and what might happen should the ice not hold. A freezing death in the churning cold water was no way to die and she shuddered at the possibility that they might not reach the other bank.

But there was no time to worry over the possibility of freezing in a river when they must first maneuver through the ranks of Stephen's army. She took one last look at the keep before Reynard took hold of her hand, gave her a quick kiss, and then pulled her through the gate. The last chance to change her mind was gone in an instant and she now had no choice but to follow her husband and the men who began tiptoeing through the forces that were surrounding them.

Elysande could barely breathe, terrified as she was that at any moment they would be discovered. She also couldn't stop shivering, both from fear and from the bitter cold that began to seep into the hem of her gown as she trudged through the snow-covered ground. No man in his right mind would be out in weather such as this, and Elysande should not be surprised that they began to easily make their way around the camp of invaders. No doubt Stephen's soldiers were huddled away in what shelter they could find.

And then the unthinkable occurred when a knight stepped from his tent, bumping straight into Richard.

"You!" a voice hissed.

Richard took hold of the knight and muffled the cry of alarm by placing his hand over the knight's mouth.

The empress stepped forward. "This knight…he is known to you, Grancourt?" she softly asked before looking in every direction for another knight to jump out at them.

"Aye, my Empress, and *he* is a *she*," Richard answered, taking a firm hold of the woman.

Reynard pulled Elysande closer whilst they tried to reassess their dire situation. "Bloody hell," he murmured.

The empress looked at the young woman who glared at those around her with hatred flashing in her eyes. "This changes our plans only somewhat. Take her back to the castle, Grancourt, since you are previously acquainted with this… *lady*. Norwood, you take the lead whilst Elysande stays with me. Kennarde and Goodee can bring up the rear and watch for threats from behind."

Richard pulled the struggling woman closer before turning to Reynard. "Be as quiet as possible as sound will travel. Watch them all and above all your back."

"Aye, I will. And you do the same, brother," Reynard replied, knowing this man was just as much a brother to him as Wymar and Theobald.

They watched as Richard disappeared into the night with his lady captive and they then continued forward in the hopes that no other would decide to come out into the night at this hour. They were now one man down and thoughts of an entire army coming up against only three knights caused Elysande to once more quiver in fear. The empress took hold of her hand, and the two women held each other close as they continued to creep through the camp until they reached the edge of the river.

Blake stepped onto the ice first, bouncing up and down to test the thickness, always aware of the death that awaited them if 'twas too thin. "'Twill hold," he uttered quietly and waved his hand for the group to follow him.

Reynard held out his hand to the empress who took a hesitant step at first…but she then gave a wide smile and reached for Elysande's hand. "Let us away," she murmured, and the two women began to make their way across the frozen river.

Elysande continued to fear for her life despite the reassurance that the ice would hold. Halfway across, the ice cracked beneath her booted feet and she again held her breath and began to pray. But thankfully the ice held and soon they were across the river. No other alarms had sounded, and there was a collective sigh of relief as everyone stood on the opposite bank and peered back to what might have awaited them.

Reynard took his wife's hand. "We had best make haste. We still have a long way to go before we reach Abingdon where we may procure horses to continue onward."

Elysande continued to gaze across the river. So many enemies had been but a heartbeat away. God must surely have been on their side for the empress and her small guard to make it through unscathed. Elysande would be sure to give Him praise when she could offer up her prayers.

But the way to Abingdon was not easy, not when the heavy snow hindered their way. Their cloaks became weighed down from the wet frosty snow that seeped into the linen. Their boots were soaked and their bodies so stiff with cold that Elysande was unsure at times if she could take another step. But she reached down into the depths of her soul for inner strength. If the empress could manage this journey, then so could she.

Six miles… six long miles of silence between them. Stumbling and falling into the deep snow causing Elysande to grow even colder but eventually, they reached their objective. Reynard went to find horses so they could ride to the empress's vassal Brian fitz Count in the nearby town of Wallingford. But riding a horse proved to be almost more difficult than walking as the wind whipped against their bodies as they galloped toward Walling-ford. Elysande was never more grateful than when they reached their destination and were welcomed into a hall with a roaring fire.

Huddling under a heavy blanket, Elysande could barely talk whilst her body began to thaw from her ordeal. Brian fitz Count listened intently to the recounting of their escape.

"And you just boldly made your way through his entire en-campment?" Brian asked in obvious wonder. Even Elysande could barely believe they escaped without much incident.

The empress huffed as though she had taken a walk in a park. "'Twas nothing short of a miracle. We were only spotted by one, but that obstacle was quickly taken care of."

Brian's eyes widened. "You had the knight killed for his body to later be discovered?"

Kingsley spoke up. "Nay. Richard Grancourt took care of the matter. The two had history together apparently."

Brian shook his head in disbelief. "'Tis hard to believe you would allow a knight to live given he could have alerted the entire camp. Sounding the alarm may have led to a handsome reward for Empress Matilda's capture."

Blake took a sip of his mulled wine. "The knight happened to be a woman who has been fighting for Stephen's cause. Richard led her away to silence her."

Reynard nodded. "Aye. I did not relish being down one

knight to protect our empress but as you can see we still managed to reach here without any further trouble."

"'Tis a miracle we made it across the river," Elysande finally spoke out.

The empress patted Elysande's hand. "But we did, thankfully. Concealing ourselves with our white clothing so we could blend in with the snow was an added boon. Plus, the weather was frigid, keeping Stephen's men slumbering the night away… praise God." Everyone murmured their agreement to the empress's words.

"Where will you head next?" Brian curiously asked.

Reynard stood, knowing how exhausted Elysande was. She looked up with him with gratitude shining in her eyes. "Once we have rested, we ride for Devizes. The empress will find a safe haven there and anyone who is loyal to her will know she will travel to this stronghold."

"My house is yours for as long as you would like. 'Tis an honor to have our empress here among her people. I know you are tired, so I bid you to rest. Rooms have been prepared for you," Brian declared, snapping his fingers whilst servants appeared to take Brian's guests to their chambers.

Reynard held out his hand to Elysande and she stood to be enveloped in his warm arms. Following the servant up the stairs to the third floor of the keep, the door was opened for them. Once they stepped inside, Reynard shut out the world so that they were alone. Elysande gave a happy sob of relief and flung herself into Reynard's arms.

"I have never been so scared in my entire life," she cried whilst Reynard's arms enveloped her.

"You are safe now, my love," he whispered resting his chin on the top of her head. "I am so proud of you. You never once complained even after you fell so many times in the snow."

A light laugh escaped her. "I could not complain… not when the empress was depending on me. I am just thankful I was not left behind and that we were not found out."

"We can give thanks to a higher being come the morn. For now, let us undress and crawl into that bed."

Elysande gave a contented sigh. "I never thought a bed could look so inviting for anything other than making love in it with my husband."

Reynard leaned down and gave her a kiss that was so enticing that Elysande began to purr, filled with a need only Reynard could fulfill. "Perchance you have a little energy left for me?" he asked with a wink.

She gave him a wicked smile. "Why, you must have read my mind, my love," she answered, pulling at his tunic to reveal his bare chest.

Their clothes began to find a place on one part of the floor after another until they were writhing together on the bed. Their lovemaking was fierce as though there was an urgency to reach their climax after all they had endured. As Reynard took her higher into the heavens above, she shattered like a burst of white-hot lightning brightening an evening sky She called out his name and in turn he, too, found his release.

And when their breathing finally returned to normal, Reynard wrapped his arms around her, bringing Elysande into his side, her head resting on his chest where she could hear the steady beat of his heart. They found their slumber, not even realizing the new day had already dawned.

CHAPTER THIRTY-SEVEN

Devizes Castle

ONCE THE EMPRESS had regained her energy for another trek across England's frozen ground, their group rode the distance to Devizes where the empress could once again rest easy knowing she was safe. They were now far enough away that there was no threat from Stephen, so they settled in and awaited news of what was happening at Oxford. But any runner that would come bearing either good or bad tidings was also hampered by the weather. Everyone's patience was running thin, especially the empress who grew more annoyed each day.

Her husband had failed her by keeping her brother Robert far longer than was necessary in Normandy. No troops had come to her rescue, nor had she seen her brother in months. The one person she heavily relied on to carry out her campaigns had been thwarted by her own spouse who had his own agenda, caring only for conquering as much of Normandy as he could. Clearly, Geoffrey had concluded that he would never be king of England nor would Matilda ever sit upon its throne.

But when a messenger arrived that Earl Robert was almost upon Devizes' gates, the empress clapped her hands in glee. Finally, her brother had arrived, and she beckoned her most trusted knights, along with Elysande, to join her in her solar for when Robert at last appeared before her.

Reynard stood at attention up against a wall with Blake and Kingsley for company. Richard and Oswin were noticeably absent, and Reynard could only ponder his friends' fates. Had Richard made it back into Oxford Castle with his prisoner? Had the woman somehow escaped? Were Oswin, Beatrix and the Empress's other ladies safe? There were many questions that must needs be addressed and only time would tell what became of those they had left behind.

Yet still… standing here reminded Reynard of a similar situation when he had waited for his next orders. He had been bored standing there at Oxford many months ago but that trip to Bristol to exchange prisoners had also brought him to his wife. He never expected such a miracle as Elysande to be thrust so unexpectedly into his life. He would be forever grateful, but he would also like nothing more than to be released from his service to the empress so that he and Elysande could begin their lives as a married couple in their own home.

When the door to the solar ricocheted off the wall, it startled not only the empress, but Elysande who also flinched at the sound. But there was nothing to fear and Robert soon entered the room to kneel before his sister. Several others entered behind him, and the room became crowded with men.

The empress rose, taking her brother's hands and bringing him to his feet. She embraced her half-brother in a rare show of public affection before she once more took her seat.

"What kept you so long?" she asked, holding out her hand for her chalice of wine that Elysande quickly gave her. The empress took a sip of her drink and handed back the cup.

"What else?" Robert said clearly upset. "Your husband, of course. It was months before I finally learned that you had been held captive in your own keep. I was almost to Oxford when news reached me that you had escaped, you clever woman. My men and I made haste to reach here since I knew this was where you would head. Your father's castle was the perfect place to hide away until I could reach you."

"And what of Oxford? Did Stephen accept my people's surrender?" the empress inquired leaning forward in her chair.

"From what I could learn, he had little choice since you were no longer within the walls. I gathered that the terms were easy enough and did not require anyone to pledge their fealty to him. I did hear that whatever prisoners you had in your dungeon were released. Hopefully, none of them were too bent on revenge," Robert warned.

The empress scowled. "The only one of any worth was Gerold Morcant who was a traitor. I suppose that scum will crawl back to his hovel north of London to live out his days under Stephen's watchful eyes."

"You may like this bit of news…" Robert laughed whilst a chair was pulled up for him next to his sister. "Did you know there are rumors going around that say you actually scaled down the tower wall to make your escape?"

"From that height?" the empress laughed in delight. "Nay, I had not heard such fanciful talk but such news amuses me greatly. Stephen must have been furious. 'Tis almost as humorous as the tale that I was dead after Winchester and was carried away in a coffin!" Laughter filled the room.

"'Twas brilliant to make your escape in the middle of the night," Robert declared as he glanced over toward Reynard and his men.

"You might not have agreed with my plan had you been here, given we almost froze to death," the empress replied as her gaze swept the men who had traveled with Robert. "Who is that standing behind your knights?"

Robert stood. "I almost forgot. I brought you a surprise, my Empress. Step forward," Robert said, holding out his arm whilst a small boy of nine summers came into view.

"Henry!" The empress beamed in delight to see her son.

"Glad tidings to you, mother," the boy said with a bow of respect.

The empress rushed forward to bring her son into her embrace. "'Tis been so long since I have seen you. My, how you have grown." The boy began to squirm, and the empress finally released him. She turned back to her brother. "I am surprised Geoffrey allowed you to bring him to me rather than fostering our son with someone he is in an alliance with."

Robert waited for his sister to return to her chair and then he did the same. "I believe your husband is under the impression that Henry will one day be placed on the throne of England. Now was a good a time to bring him here as any."

"At least he trusted you with his care—as will I," the empress said whilst watching her son.

Robert leaned back before answering. "Aye, he did, but I am also glad that your own trusted knights saw to your welfare in my absence. They should be rewarded, and handsomely."

The empress nodded. "I have already seen that Norwood has been made lord of Blackmore and he has wed Lady Elysande as well."

"I wish you both well," Earl Robert declared, nodding in approval.

Reynard bowed. "Thank you, my lord." He took a sideways glance toward his wife who dropped into a curtsey.

The empress drummed her fingers upon the arm of her chair. "Mayhap there is more we can do for Norwood. Step forward," she called, and Reynard came to stand before his empress. Elysande appeared worried, not that he could blame her.

"My Empress," Reynard said, bowing his head.

"You and your brothers have faithfully stood by my side for many years now. Although I expect you to continue to remain loyal to my cause, I now release you from your service. You and your wife may take your leave and return home to Blackmore come the morn."

"You are too gracious, Empress," Reynard answered, watching Elysande as her smile brightened knowing they were going home.

"See well to this lady, Norwood. Although Blackmore has had many repairs since you were last there, 'twill still take many years to bring the place back to its former glory. But the keep as it is now should suffice for your needs to begin your lives together."

The empress waved her hand toward Elysande, and she quickly ran to Reynard's side. He pulled his lovely lady into his arms, raising her trembling fingertips to his lips so he could give them a kiss. They smiled together and gave a joyful laugh. They were going home!

CHAPTER THIRTY-EIGHT

Blackmore Castle

ELYSANDE TOOK HOLD of her cloak and began to make her way from her bedchamber. A rumble of male laughter filled the room when Reynard playfully grabbed her from behind. The warmth of his naked chest sent a thrill through her as it always did, making her long to return to bed with him, but there were chores that needed attending to so she could begin her day.

Reynard nuzzled her neck. "Where do you think you are headed, wife?" he purred into her ear, giving the lobe a tiny nibble.

She turned in his arms to face the man who meant all to her. "Where do you think, husband? The daily chores will not get done by themselves. You have already distracted me for nigh unto an hour with our play this morn."

He began to trail kisses down her neck and she softly sighed. "Chores can wait. I, however, cannot."

As much as she wished otherwise, she would have to deny him. "Tell that to the cow waiting to be milked in our stable. I swear I can hear the poor animal bellowing her discomfort from here," she said whilst running her fingers over his muscled chest.

"'Tis just a cow, Elysande, and the empress sent enough servants that any one of them can see to the animals in the stable. How can you deny me when the bed awaits our pleasure?" he replied, and the husky baritone of his voice almost convinced her to stay.

"Deny you? Surely you jest with me, my lord, for did we not just tumble between the linens once… nay… twice this morn?" she teased, giving him a quick kiss.

He gave a heavy sigh. "Then if you must go, wait for me to finish dressing and I will accompany you."

She raised her hand to cup his cheek. "I am certain you can survive a few minutes without me. Take your time and meet me in the stables when you are ready."

"We have servants now for that, Elysande," he reminded her again.

"Some habits are hard to let go of." She gave him a bright smile.

"I will miss you," he murmured and bent forward to seal his words with a long kiss.

She could not deny him another kiss and more minutes passed before he at last allowed her to find her voice and continue their conversation. "I will not be gone from your company for long." Her arm wound around his neck, and she held him to her as though he was the only reason she remained upright. A moan left him when his tongue began to dance with her own again and she finally had to give a push against his chest to remember what was required of her.

Her breathing was ragged, and she wished she could take her husband up on the offer of the pleasure she would receive if she only gave into his demands. "You are trying to distract me again," she whispered, twirling a dark strand of his hair between her fingers.

"Is it working, my love?" he asked with a roguish grin.

"If only…"

"Are you certain?" Reynard once again pulled her up against his rock-hard body causing parts of her to swoon from the heat radiating from him.

She waved one finger at him. "Stop tempting me, Reynard," she teased although she was certain her eyes sparkled in delight. What wife would not be pleased that her husband wished to keep her in their bedchamber?

"Then go if you must but know that I am not happy you are not giving in to my demands." He finally released her and as she turned, he playfully swatted her bottom.

She abruptly twirled back around only to see his amusement upon his visage. "Really? Is this how our lives together are to be?" she teased whilst rubbing her only slightly abused backside.

"Most likely, but feel free to stay here with me in order to make it up to me," he said laughing.

"I am the one who has a sore bottom. Do you not think *you* should be the one to apologize?"

He stepped forward and kissed the tip of her nose. "Apologize? I believe, little one, I was thinking of something more than just having speech together."

There was a promise lingering in his gaze, and she wished with all her heart she could give in to his offer. But she could imagine the loud bellow in the distance, and she could not put off her chores any longer.

"Later?" she asked in a seductive whisper that had him pulling her up against his erect manhood.

"Most definitely, my lady," he growled in what sounded like complete anguish.

"Do not worry, my lord. You shall survive the briefest of partings until I can see to *your* needs again," she called over her shoulder as she headed toward the door.

A chuckle left him. "Then you best take care of that blasted cow quickly, wife, because I shall be down to the stables shortly. I believe there's a nice new pile of straw in the loft that might suffice for a bed."

"You are impossible."

"Aye," he said grinning, "but you love me anyway."

"Aye… that I do. I shall see you shortly."

Elysande watched him give a short nod before he turned and went to a table that held several parchments for him to read. He would be busy far longer than he intended if he were to peruse all that required his own attention as lord of the keep.

Closing the door behind her, she made her way to one of the turrets to descend into her hall. One day, she would create beautiful tapestries that would grace the walls to replace the ones that had been burned by Stephen's men. She shook her head at the thought of the damage they had created months ago. She should not look to the past but only to her future with Reynard. There was much to look forward to now that they had returned home.

Aye… who would have known when Reynard stumbled upon her at her grandfather's gravesite, that she would eventually set aside her misgivings for the young knight and fall in love with him? He was an unexpected blessing and she had much to be thankful for. She would remind him each and every day how he had stolen her heart almost from the very beginning.

She swung around in joy that she was home and was very much loved. Quickly, she grabbed a hold of a bit of cheese and bread that was sitting on one of the tables, nodded to one of the servants serving the knights who had returned to Blackmore, and then hurried out the keep's front door. The heavy wood banged shut behind her as she scurried to reach the barn and the animals who were needing to be taken care of. She knew these simple chores she had once performed should be a thing of her past. After all, she was now lady of the keep—and as Reynard had mentioned, she had servants to see to the animals in the stable. On the morrow, she would set in place arrangements for others to handle this from now on.

She had just reached the barn and rounded the corner to head toward the door when she was once again grabbed from behind. 'Twas a firmer grip than she was used to with their play, and she could not help but flinch at the unexpected unpleasantness of Reynard's touch. He had never hurt her before.

"Easy, Reynard, else you will bruise me all over," she huffed, trying to face him to no avail. But she froze in fear a moment later when the voice that reached her ears was not the sound of her beloved husband.

"Did you miss me, my pet?" the voice asked as he inhaled the scent of her hair. She was immediately spun around so she could face her tormentor.

"You!" she cried upon seeing the face of none other than Gerold Morcant. Any thoughts the empress may have had that this miscreant would hide himself away were proven false for he stood here before her.

"Aye! Me. And this time you will not get away so easily. You and that whoreson Norwood owe me," Morcant promised as he put his gloved hand over her mouth so she could not scream.

Elysande tried to dig the heels of her boots into the dirt, but he continued to pull her along until they reached his horse. As he made quick work of gagging and binding her, she could only ponder why these things kept happening to her. When he tossed her up onto his horse, she tried to jump back down but Morcant was too quick for her. With her held in his tight grip, Morcant took up the reins and put his heels into the horse's side.

Before she could fully comprehend what was happening, Morcant was galloping out the unmanned gate of Blackmore. She could only wonder how long 'twould be before her husband realized she was gone.

CHAPTER THIRTY-NINE

ALMOST AN HOUR had passed since Elysande had left their bedchamber. Reynard swiped his hand over eyes to help clear his vision. He swore all the numbers the steward had written down had begun to run together until he could not look upon the ledger any longer. Time to reward himself for his labors by finding his wife. A wicked grin spread across his mouth as he thought of what they might do together. She was a fast learner as to what he liked and from the moans of pleasure that had come from her, Reynard was well aware that she had walked from this room satisfied. But hopefully enough time had passed to reignite her appetite again.

Knowing what he promised her and what awaited him in their stables, he quickly left the room and went in search of his wife. He nodded to several knights who continued to break their fast in the great hall, thankful several had returned to guard Blackmore from invaders. But their numbers were still low, and Reynard realized he might need to petition the empress for more men if he were to hold the fortress in her name.

A servant came and brought him a bowl of porridge that he quickly ate before deciding Elysande had had enough time to take care of the animals who needed to be fed. He left the keep and began making his way toward the stables. He frowned when he witnessed odd marks in the dirt when he neared the door, wondering what had been dragged with such force. He opened the door and peered into the dark interior. The smell of hay and manure was strong. He would need to ensure the stalls were given a thorough cleaning now that they had plenty of servants to see to such matters.

"Elysande," he called, searching for his wife and not espying her. The stall with the cow was empty. In fact, a small stool and an empty bucket stood at the entrance, giving evidence that Elysande had not even completed the main reason she came to the stable. The cow bellowed in protest.

"Elysande, where are you?" he yelled, thinking she was hiding and waiting for him to find her. He searched the other empty stalls and even the loft but his wife was nowhere to be found.

This did not bode well. His lady would not just disappear of her own accord, nor would she fail to complete her morning tasks unless something or someone disturbed her. He left the stable and once more searched the surrounding area. Nothing. No sound of his wife and nothing to determine where she was.

His attention returned to the marks in the ground, and he followed them around the stable. A frown marred his brow when he saw the hoof prints of a horse. Panic set in when he began to realize someone had most likely taken his wife. A servant came into the bailey, and Reynard pointed him back to the keep.

"Get my knights. Someone has taken Lady Elysande," he ordered as he ran back to the stable to saddle his horse. He made quick work of securing the cinches and attaching the bridle before tightening the clasp on his belt that held his scabbard. He then easily leapt into the saddle. He was just maneuvering his steed through the door when four knights came charging toward him.

"Make haste, men, and follow me as you can. I must find who has taken my wife," Reynard ordered whilst his horse reared up on its back hooves. The men backed away from the animal whilst Reynard gained control of his mount.

"Wait for us, my lord. 'Tis dangerous for you to leave alone," one knight proclaimed.

"I can take care of myself but hurry. I cannot delay any longer and must needs save my lady," Reynard replied before he pressed his knees into the side of his horse that bolted forward.

He was more or less blind when it came to determining where Elysande had been taken, or by whom. He could only pray that he was going the right way. And then miracle of all miracles, he saw a piece of blue linen that had found its way onto a bush by the side of the road. He halted his horse and took the fabric in his fingers. His wife was such a clever woman. She was leaving him a trail to follow!

He rode onward for mayhap another five miles before he found himself at a cross road. His choice of path would either bring him closer to his wife or farther away. He stood questioning which way he should take when a distant shriek toward the road on the left made him slap the reins of the bridle to tear off in that direction. Clearly, his wife was in trouble and was making an attempt to protect herself. He prayed with all his heart that she would be able to hold out just a little bit longer and that he would reach her soon enough.

When he rounded a corner, there she stood. The sight that met his eyes was almost more than Reynard could stand. Her black hair was disheveled, her gown torn from her attempts to leave him markers to follow. But 'twas the fact she held a knife out in front of her and had to use it that made Reynard's heart sink. That never should have happened—he should have been there to defend her himself. But at least she had the blade. He remembered when he had instructed her to always keep one hidden in her boot. She had at the very least listened for a change and 'twas clear that the knife had come in handy.

"You bloody bitch," Morcant yelled whilst holding a cloth to his bleeding cheek.

"Put your hands on me again and I will scar the other," Elysande warned, swiping the blade back and forth.

"I will teach you a lesson you will soon not forget," Morcant said, taking a menacing step forward.

'Twas obvious the two combatants were too engrossed in each other to realize they were no longer alone.

"I think not, Morcant. Stay away from my wife," Reynard declared, bringing his horse forward and then jumping down. He drew his sword from his scabbard and held the blade in front of him.

"Reynard," Elysande sobbed. "You came for me."

Reynard lifted one brow, then gave her a wink. "You had your doubts? You and I have unfinished business, if you recall."

A roar of outrage left Morcant, and his blade rang out as it met Reynard's. The two men began to fight, their swords flashing in the brightness of the sun. Elysande stepped out of the way and Reynard gave his full concentration to the foe before him. In terms of skill, he was no different than any enemy that Reynard had met on the battlefield, but never before had any foe stirred in him such a fierce rage. 'Twas this man who had taken his wife!

He heard a rustling behind him and in his haste to turn and check on Elysande's state, he let his guard drop in a moment of distraction. A moment his enemy capitalized on, as Morcant's blade sliced across his arm, causing Reynard to curse. But this only renewed his determination to see that Morcant did not live to see another day. The empress may have kept him a prisoner in his dungeon but Reynard would not be so lenient.

"I should have killed you the first chance I had on the tourney field," Morcant taunted.

"You failed in your attempts then just as you shall fail this day." Reynard swung his blade forward, attacking the man before him with renewed strength.

"If I had taken her to my bed, she would be my wife," Morcant taunted, flinching when Reynard's sword sliced into his thigh.

"Then you and I would not be here this day for you would have been dead as soon as I could hunt you down, punished you for the crime of taking someone who does not belong to you," Reynard hissed, pressing forward.

"I will see you dead," Morcant said through clenched teeth.

"You can try but in the end I will be the one walking away

with the lady," Reynard said, slicing his blade again and again as Morcant began to bleed from several wounds.

Morcant whirled around to evade Reynard's sword but when he brought his own forward to strike a killing blow, Reynard ducked down, pulled his own knife from his boot, and struck upward to pierce Morcant directly in the middle of his chest. Morcant's eyes went wide in disbelief before he stumbled backwards.

"You b-bastard," Morcant stammered.

"I hope you enjoy your stay in hell, Morcant. The Devil will be waiting for your arrival," Reynard sneered as he watched his enemy fall onto the ground. He went over to the fallen man to ensure he was dead, pushing the body with his boot to see if there was any flinch of response. But Morcant was no more and could only stare upwards with sightless eyes.

Reynard wiped his sword on Morcant's tunic before putting his faithful blade away. He then held open his arms and Elysande ran to him. He swore from that day forward, he would never allow this lady to be far from his side.

CHAPTER FORTY

ELYSANDE SLAMMED OPEN the keep door, swiftly hastened through the inner bailey, and pressed onward until she reached the field where Reynard and the few knights who guarded Blackmore were training. She took in great gulps of air to calm her frayed nerves. After almost a fortnight of peace, there was an army approaching. Elysande had marched up the turret stairs to see for herself the dust plume in the distance from the battlement walls. Whether friend or foe, she could not tell but Reynard must be warned in case 'twas Stephen's men bent on causing more havoc on their home.

But as urgent as the matter was, she did not lose sight of the fact that her husband was sparring with naked blades. Startling him or his training partner could lead to an injury she would much sooner avoid. Thus, she waited for the opportunity when she could interrupt without causing trouble. The knight he was sparring with fell upon the ground, giving her the perfect chance.

"Reynard," she called, waving her hand with a renewed sense of urgency.

He took off his helmet and pushed back the mail coif from his head. Placing his sword in his scabbard, he began to approach. He was an impressive sight to her eyes and her breath hitched as it usually did the closer he came. He was a warrior in every sense of the word and the chain mail links chinked with each step he took.

"*Mon amour*," he whispered in a soft accent before bending forward to seal a kiss upon her lips.

She would have lost herself in the moment if not for the danger that approached. "There are men drawing near. Too many to count but from what I could see from the battlements, they have only one destination in mind."

Reynard swore beneath his breath and called out to the men to take their places to guard the gate. He took Elysande's hand and together they began to make their way back toward the keep. "You will go inside until I come for you."

"I will not leave your side," she said instead of obeying him.

"Must this always be an argument between us?" he asked with a scowl. "I cannot concentrate on guarding our lands if I must needs be worrying over your safety."

"Then you should have listened to me when I asked you to teach me how to defend myself with a sword," she huffed, placing her hands on her hips.

Reynard rolled his eyes. "The blade I asked the smithy to make for you is almost done but you will need several years of practice in wielding it before I am confident enough that you can stand by my side in a battle."

She looked toward the weak defenses near where the barbican gate would one day be in place again. "Do you think that barrier will hold?"

He ran his hand through his hair before he pulled the coif back into place. "Nay, I do not but I will not let the few knights we have be slaughtered if the approaching army will do us harm. I must go to fight with them. Now, please go inside and be safe."

She saw his logic even if she still did not want to part from his side. "Please take care, my love." She pulled on his surcote to kiss him. His gauntlet hand pulled her against the hardness of his body, and she could feel the chainmail beneath his garment. The kiss was brief before he tore his lips away and gave her a gentle push toward the keep's door. His command was silent but unmistakable, and she could do nothing else but tear herself away from his side.

She had just placed her hand on the handle of the keep door

when a lone rider approached the gate. Elysande raised her hand to shield her eyes from the sunlight to peer at the man who jumped down from his horse. He tore the helmet from his head and recognition made her heart leap with joy.

"Hawke!" Elysande called out. She heard her husband give a short chuckle before she began running toward her captain. Once she reached him, she jumped into his arms and heard his grunt of surprise.

"Did you miss me, my lady?" he laughed, twirling her around before he set her back down on her feet. He remembered himself and gave her a short bow of respect.

"You finally found your way home," she beamed happily as Reynard joined her and held out his hand.

"Welcome back," Reynard said as the two men clasped forearms.

"'Tis good to be home… that is, if you shall still have me," Hawke declared, looking at the pair.

Reynard chuckled. "Of course, you are always welcome here. Someone has to help me keep an eye on this lady. She continues to get into all sorts of mischief, causing havoc in my life."

Elysande playfully swatted her husband. "'Tis not my fault men continue to try to abduct me. Besides, I am not the one people call the Knight of Havoc."

Hawke raised a brow at their words. "I sense a story here somewhere, but I suppose that can wait until later. The empress has sent you a whole garrison of men to help you protect these lands in her name. And your maid Olive is somewhere in the center. She was not happy to be left behind at Oxford and was only too willing to return with us to serve you as soon as we were able to travel."

Elysande widened her eyes. "How shall we feed them all through the rest of winter?" she asked, mentally tallying the food stores they currently had.

Hawke held up his hand. "No need to worry, Lady Elysande. The empress has thought of that too. There are several wagons of supplies that will come in handy until the fields can be planted again come the spring."

Reynard placed his hand on Hawke's shoulder. "Go see to your horse and we shall have Cook prepare a feast for tonight to welcome those who will now serve Blackmore."

Elysande watched Hawke take the reins of his horse and began leading the animal toward the stable. Once Reynard gave orders to the men standing at the gate, they made their way inside the keep. Elysande instructed the kitchen servants to prepare more for the evening meal and asked for a tub to be filled with water in their chamber so her husband could bathe after his training.

She had hoped to see to him personally, but one servant after another demanded her attention for instructions regarding the number of people who would now inhabit Blackmore for the foreseeable future. After almost an hour, she was finally able to make her way up the turret stairs, down the passageway, and to open the door to her bedchamber. Her hand firmly gripped the handle at the sight of her naked husband. A boy was standing on a stool and pouring rinse water over Reynard's head.

She swallowed hard whilst entering the room. "You may leave us," she told the boy who jumped off the stool, put the bucket down and quickly left the lord and the lady. Reynard stepped from the tub and Elysande took a linen and began wiping dry his dripping wet body. He shook his head, sending water flying, causing her to laugh. He pulled her close.

"You could have waited so I did not become as wet as you," she teased whilst the towel was wrenched from her hands. He tossed it aside.

"What took you so long? I had hoped you would join me whilst I bathed." He began nuzzling her neck as he began walking her backwards toward their bed.

"Duty called," she said, placing her hands on his shoulders and stroking his hot skin.

"Your lord and husband says that there is but one duty that

demands your attention."

She raised her eyes and took her finger to her chin as though contemplating her many options. "You do not think this could wait considering we most likely have a whole garrison of knights you must needs address and see settled?" she mocked with what she hoped were mischievous eyes.

"I have waited long enough," he purred into her ear. He took hold of her gown and raised it up over her head. Her undergarments followed until she was as naked as he was. He laid her down and they sank into the feather mattress.

"I waited an entire lifetime to find you," she murmured, taking hold of one of his dark brown locks of hair and twirling it between her fingertips.

He stroked her tresses until he cupped her cheek. "As did I for you, dearest wife. In case I did not tell you this today, I love you."

Her heart soared at his words. "As I love you, although you may have to prove it to me to ensure I do not forget."

A low laugh rumbled in his chest. "Now *that* is a command I will gladly obey."

And obey he did, far into the afternoon hour and for many years to come. She had found the one man who made her complete and they had a lifetime before them to look forward to. Blackmore would thrive under Reynard's command and if they were so blessed, children would follow to carry on their name.

Aye... Elysande was more than content to have Reynard Norwood as her husband. She no longer had to worry how she might defend her home, not with one of the empress's finest knights as Blackmore's protector. She had found her true home in Reynard's arms. She was indeed blessed.

EPILOGUE

Blackmore Castle, England
Summer, 1146

R EYNARD PACED HIS solar with worry. It had been hours since Elysande had begun having pains to announce the birth of their second child. His brothers had attempted to distract him with food and wine but everything they tried to feed him was tasteless. How could he eat or drink when the moans of the torture Elysande was enduring could be heard echoing down the hallways? He swore he would never touch her again so she would not have to be put in such pain.

Wymar slammed his cup upon the table before him. "For God's sake, brother, sit," he demanded whilst raking his hand through his light brown hair.

Theobald nodded. "Aye. You are making me dizzy watching you pace back and forth. Your wife might still be in labor for hours so you might as well enjoy a cup of wine and make merry. You are, after all, about to become a father again."

Reynard growled an oath in frustration. "I do not know how the two of you have been able to remain so calm," he grumbled. "Can you not listen to what I am putting my wife through?"

The two men gave each other a knowing look before Wymar spoke first. "I recall being in the same state, more so with the first child."

"Aye," Theobald chimed in, "but this is your second so you should have already been prepared for what awaited you. Soon your daughter will have a sibling to torture as he or she grows."

Wymar laughed. "Aye! Much like I had the pleasure of making both your lives miserable when we were children."

"Sod off, both of you, or you will drive me mad," Reynard cursed, reaching for his wine and finally taking a sip.

Wymar raised his cup to salute the two men. "To my brothers and the women who make our lives all the better."

Theobald raised his chalice. "I shall drink to that!"

Reynard returned the salute and took another drink, but his cup rattled upon the table when the door was thrust open and Olive poked her head in with a smile.

"Is she…" Reynard began praying he had not lost his wife in the birthing process.

"Well and waiting for you, milord," the girl said with a bright smile.

That was all Reynard had to hear as he ran from the solar to reach his bedchamber down the passageway. The door was already ajar and inside Wymar's wife, Ceridwen, was wrapping a child in clean linen. Theobald's wife, Ingrid, was holding the hand of Reynard's oldest child who was sucking her thumb.

When the girl saw him standing at the door, she wobbled over on unsteady legs and held up her hands for him to lift her. "Up," she demanded.

Reynard smiled, knowing he could not deny Serena any more than he could deny her mother. He lifted the girl, and she patted his cheeks before he gave her a quick kiss on her own. "Go with your Aunt Ingrid, my sweet, and your papa will see you later."

Ingrid came over and took Serena. "Congratulations on the birth of your child, Reynard," she said with a smile.

"A boy or girl?" he asked.

"Aye," she said laughing not answering him.

Ceridwen placed the child in Elysande's waiting arms before also coming toward the door. She kissed his cheek. "We shall let your wife tell you of your child," she answered before she shooed out the remaining servants and left them to their privacy.

Reynard quickly made his way to gently sit on the edge of their bed. "Are you well?"

Elysande gave him a tired smile. "'Twas more difficult than when I birthed Serena, but we managed."

"I will never put you through this again," he vowed, leaning forward to kiss her forehead.

"Aye, you will, my dearest love. I think we shall have many more children to fill our hall," she whispered. "Would you like to hold your son?"

A son! So many thoughts swarmed through his head at the thought of a son to carry on his name and the title the empress had given him. Elysande was still waiting until he held out his hands and the small babe was placed in his arms. He pulled back the edge of the linens to reveal a crop of black hair upon the tiny infant's head, reminding him of the child's mother.

"He is beautiful, just as you are, my love," he replied whilst Elysande moved over to make room for Reynard to join her on the bed.

He placed the child between them so they could unwrap the cloth and closely inspect the baby.

Elysande bent down and kissed the infant's downy head. "He is perfect. Ten toes… ten fingers. He will become strong just like his father one day."

Reynard began covering the child again whilst Elysande gave a yawn. "I am so proud of you, Elysande."

"As long as you are happy with the child…"

"Happy? Oh, aye! I am very happy with our son, wife." He picked up the child and stood to rock back and forth upon his feet. "He will be a champion knight for the empress and her son Henry one day."

Elysande laughed. "Well, mayhap we could get him walking before he pledges his fealty to the monarchy. What shall we call him?"

Reynard pondered the small child he held in his arms. The world would one day be at this boy's feet. "We shall name him

Dristan… Dristan of Blackmore."

"A fitting name for a champion knight," Elysande declared with another yawn.

Reynard returned to sit again on the edge of the bed. "Thank you for our son."

His wife reached over to pat his hand. "Thank you for loving me."

He leaned forward to kiss her lips and heard her sigh of contentment. "I will always love you, Elysande. Forever and always will our souls be bound together.

"Aye… for all eternity will our love survive," she said softly as her eyes began to close in sleep.

"Rest, my lovely wife, and dream of us. I will see to our son," Reynard replied and soon his wife drifted off to sleep.

He rose and went to the shutter to open the latch so the last rays of the evening sun shone into the room. He lifted his child so the sunbeams graced the boy. "Welcome to the light, Dristan of Blackmore."

The boy opened his eyes. Reynard swore he saw his own grey ones staring back at him before the child yawned much like his mother moments ago, falling back asleep. Reynard placed his son in the small cradle they had waiting for him in their room. He then made his way back to his wife and laid down next to her. She immediately was drawn into his embrace and snuggled in her place with her head resting on his chest.

He gave a heavy, contented sigh. His life could not be any more perfect. A wife who fulfilled his every need and desire. A daughter and a son to carry on his name and perchance more if they were so blessed. His brothers and their wives also happily married with children of their own. Reynard was not sure how they had all been so blessed, but he would thank the good Lord above come the morn. He had much to be thankful for.

And as he, too, began to drift off to sleep with his wife lying next to him, he realized that Elysande had made a home for him here within the walls of Blackmore Castle. A castle that they would continue to fill with love and their children. His days of being called the Knight of Havoc were now over. He had many years to relish in the idea that he was loved by a woman who made his heart sing. He could not ask for anything more.

THE END

Sherry Ewing needs your help!

Book reviews help readers to find books, and authors to find readers. Please consider writing a review for ***Knight of Havoc***; even a few sentences telling people what you liked about the story is helpful. Reviews can be posted on BookBub, Goodreads, and Amazon. Thank you for purchasing and reading a copy of ***Knight of Havoc***. I hope you enjoyed Reynard and Elysande's journey to finding love.

For links to this book, see Sherry's website at
www.sherryewing.com/books

AUTHOR NOTE

Dearest Reader:

Thank you so very much for purchasing a copy of **Knight of Havoc**. I hope you enjoyed the third book in my *Knights of the Anarchy* series!

I have to admit it… I had a very big author moment when I wrote the end of this book. I had been envisioning this part of the Norwood brothers' series for years. But when Reynard named his child Dristan of Blackmore, a very pivotal moment occurred, tying this series in with my first self-published book, **If My Heart Could See You: The MacLarens (Book One)**. I had never mentioned much of Dristan's parents, and now here we are coming full circle. When an author cries over her own work, well… it's a super good moment.

As I just mentioned, I knew the ending of this story for years, but I found that I had written myself into a bit of a pickle because of the timeframe I needed in order to have everything work out with the birth of Dristan. In 1142 during the Anarchy, there weren't a lot of battles going on like in **Knight of Darkness** or **Knight of Chaos**. I knew I wanted the main conflict to mostly be centered around the siege at Oxford but that was over a whole year away from when I'd left my characters.

I centered the beginning of this book with Reynard heading to Bristol and then back to Winchester for the exchange of prisoners—King Stephen and the empress's half-brother Earl Robert. Considering all the conflict between these two entities, the exchange was far more peaceful than anyone expected.

The empress did take up residence at Oxford. However, the tournament depicted in my story was fictional on my part to move the plot forward and to introduce more characters vying for Elysande's hand. It should be noted that during this time period, England's people were struggling to make ends meet. The war had indeed taken a toll on its people who were starving and mostly tired of a war that had raged for years.

I once again relied heavily on a research book entitled *Matilda: Empress. Queen. Warrior.* by Catherine Hanley. There's only so much you can learn on the internet, and I have found this book about Empress Matilda's life fascinating. She was an incredible woman who unfortunately never sat on the throne but ended up claiming it through her son, Henry II.

Thank you to Kathryn Le Veque and the whole Dragonblade Publishing team for all your hard work to see this book published. I am humbly grateful to everyone involved in this project.

Thank you to my incredible editor Elizabeth Mazer who continues to work with me on making my books better for my readers. I can only hope you never leave me! Thank you to the moon and back, Elizabeth.

I always have to give thanks to my family for putting up with me and all my stress when I'm getting close to a deadline. A special thanks to my daughter Jessica. She continues to be my sounding board when I get stuck in a plot hole. She's also responsible for Elysande's name. She certainly likes the unusual.

And last but certainly not least, thank you to all my readers both new and those who have been with me from the very beginning. There are not enough words to express my gratitude for all your support and what you do on my behalf. Never forget you are the reason I continue to write, and you all have a special place in my heart.

I hope you enjoyed Reynard and Elysande's journey to finding love. You'll see Richard's story **Knight of Mayhem** next and the heroine who I slipped into this story at Oxford. Until the next time, take care and keep on reading!

With much love,
Sherry

OTHER BOOKS BY SHERRY EWING

Medieval & Time Travel Series

Knight of Darkness: The Knights of the Anarchy (Book One)
Sometimes finding love can become our biggest weakness…

Knight of Chaos: The Knights of the Anarchy (Book Two)
In the chaos of war, can one knight defy the odds to find peace
with the woman warrior he loves?

Knight of Havoc: The Knights of the Anarchy (Book Three)
One lone knight. One strongminded maiden. When duty wars
with love at first sight, which will win?

To Love A Scottish Laird: De Wolfe Pack Connected World
Sometimes you really can fall in love at first sight…

To Love An English Knight: De Wolfe Pack Connected World
Can a chance encounter lead to love?

*If My Heart Could See You: The MacLarens, A Medieval Romance
(Book One)*
When you're enemies, does love have a fighting chance?

*For All of Ever: The Knights of Berwyck, A Quest Through Time
(Book One)*
Sometimes to find your future, you must look to the past…

*Only For You: The Knights of Berwyck, A Quest Through Time
(Book Two)*
Sometimes it's hard to remember that true love conquers all, only

after the battle is over…

Hearts Across Time: The Knights of Berwyck (Books One & Two)
Sometimes all you need is to just believe… _Hearts Across Time_ is a special edition box set that combines Katherine and Riorden's stories together from _For All of Ever_ and _Only For You._

A Knight To Call My Own: The MacLarens, A Medieval Romance (Book Two)
When your heart is broken, is love still worth the risk?

To Follow My Heart: The Knights of Berwyck, A Quest Through Time (Book Three)
Love is a leap. Sometimes you need to jump…

The Piper's Lady: The MacLarens, A Medieval Romance (Book Three)
True love binds them. Deceit divides them. Will they choose love?

Love Will Find You: The Knights of Berwyck, A Quest Through Time (Book Four)
Sometimes a moment is all we have…

One Last Kiss: The Knights of Berwyck, A Quest Through Time (Book Five)
Sometimes it takes a miracle to find your heart's desire…

Promises Made At Midnight: The Knights of Berwyck, A Quest Through Time (Book Six)
Make a wish…

It Began With A Kiss: The MacLarens, A Medieval Romance (Book Four)
Sometimes you need to listen when your heart begins to sing…

Regency

A Kiss For Charity: A de Courtenay Novella (Book One)
Love heals all wounds but will their pride keep them apart?

The Earl Takes A Wife: A de Courtenay Novella (Book Two)
It began with a memory, etched in the heart.

Before I Found You: A de Courtenay Novella (Book Three)
A quest for a title. An encounter with a stranger. Will she choose
love?

Nothing But Time: A Family of Worth (Book One)
They will risk everything for their forbidden love…

One Moment In Time: A Family of Worth (Book Two)
One moment in time may be enough, if it lasts forever…

A Love Beyond Time: A Family of Worth (Book Three) in the
Bluestocking Belles *Under the Harvest Moon* 2023 boxset
Can love at first sight be reborn after heartbreak, proving a
second chance is all you need?

Under the Mistletoe
A new suitor seeks her hand. An old flame holds her heart. Which
one will she meet under the kissing bough?

A Mistletoe Kiss in the Bluestocking Belles boxset *Belles & Beaux*
(2022)
All she wants for Christmas is a mistletoe kiss…

A Second Chance At Love
Can the bittersweet frost of lost love be rekindled into a burning
flame?

A Countess to Remember
Sometimes love finds you when you least expect it…

To Claim A Lyon's Heart: Lyon's Den Connected World
A gambler's bet. A widow's burden. Will one game of chance
change their lives?

The Lyon and His Promise: Lyon's Den Connected World
A gentleman's lifetime regret. A widow's tarnished reputation.
Can they repair the past to create a bright future together?

You can find out more about Sherry's work on her website at
www.SherryEwing.com and at online retailers.

SOCIAL MEDIA FOR SHERRY EWING

You can learn more about Sherry Ewing at these social media links:

Amazon Author Page: amzn.to/1TrWtoy

Bookbub: bookbub.com/authors/sherry-ewing

Dragonblade Publishing: dragonbladepublishing.com/team/sherry-ewing

Facebook: facebook.com/SherryEwingAuthor

Goodreads: goodreads.com/author/show/8382315.Sherry_Ewing

Instagram: instagram.com/sherry.ewing

Pinterest: pinterest.com/SherryLEwing

TikTok: tiktok.com/@sherryewingauthor

X: @Sherry_Ewing

YouTube: youtube.com/SherryEwingauthor

Newsletter Sign Up: bit.ly/2vGrqQM

Facebook Street Team: facebook.com/groups/799623313455472

Facebook Official Fan Page: facebook.com/groups/356905935241836

ABOUT SHERRY EWING

Sherry Ewing picked up her first historical romance when she was a teenager and has been hooked ever since. An award-winning and bestselling author, she writes historical and time travel romances to awaken the soul one heart at a time. When not writing, she can be found in the San Francisco Bay Area at her day job as an Information Technology Specialist.

Learn more about Sherry where a new adventure awaits you on every page:
Website: www.SherryEwing.com
Email: Sherry@SherryEwing.com